# TAKEN:
## A TERRAMATES NOVEL

### LISA LACE

TAKEN
Copyright © 2015 Toppings Publishing.
All rights reserved.

**Disclaimer**

This book is licensed for your personal enjoyment only.

**Copyright Notes**

# CONTENTS

# CHAPTER 1

Lyzette tottered down the street in her high heels. She was late and trying to hurry, but it was a losing battle in her four-inch spikes and short red skirt. The tight blouse that showed off her ample cleavage didn't impede her walking although it made breathing difficult. Every time she inhaled, she felt constrained.

She darted as quickly as she could across the busy street, taking her life in her hands as she jaywalked across four lanes of traffic. On the other side of the road, she nearly toppled over. A thoughtful man in a black suit saved her. He reached out to steady her as she stepped up onto the sidewalk. She gave him a genuine smile. He gave her an odd leer that made her feel uncomfortable. Men ogled Lyzette all the time, and she didn't think much of it.

The cars buzzed past her. Lyzette longed to have enough credits to take a car, instead of having to walk and ride the subway. She'd have enough someday. She watched as a good looking couple got in one, programmed it, and turned to talk to each other as the car sped away to their destination.

Perhaps she could have chosen more practical clothes, but it was too late to think of that now. She felt she would have more power if she wore high heels and clothes that made her look good, but it never worked for her. She hadn't been able to get life to go her way, even when she tried her hardest. Maybe today would be different.

She continued walking towards the skyscraper, thinking about her problems getting a job. They started from high school. The only reason she had a diploma was because her uncle had bullied the principal. Her first two jobs ended with her getting fired. Her best friend had said she wasn't a good fit for the companies. Her best friend was a kind person. Lyzette knew better.

They told her she wasn't smart enough. She wasn't skilled enough. There were plenty of girls that were prettier. One thing that was good enough was her body. Men always liked her curvy hips and full bosom — they liked getting their hands on them. But she hadn't given away her most precious jewel yet. She was saving that for her husband. She had messed around with guys a lot, but she had never let them go all the way.

Lyzette had always thought she would be able to land a husband when she was younger. She wasn't sure anymore. The guys she dated all wanted one thing from her, and when she couldn't give it to them, they drifted away.

It was enough to drive a girl insane.

But she had decided she wasn't going to go crazy trying to figure out how to get married. She was going to get a career. That's why she was dressed up. She was going to a job interview for an administrative assistant position.

Lyzette excelled at typing, and she could answer the phone. She could do a fantastic job, and she would focus on that and forget about men.

An hour later, she was perched on a couch in the president's office, keeping her knees together as her mother had taught her and sitting up nice and straight. She had been answering questions for about five minutes when Mr. Loder came over and sat down next to her on the couch. He was sitting a little too close, and she felt uncomfortable. She was afraid to say anything because he might be her future boss.

"Lyzette, do you want to be my assistant?" he asked.

"Yes," she said, nodding her head decisively, trying to look like a career woman.

"What would you be willing to do to get that kind of good paying job?" he asked again, putting his hand on her leg and sliding it up. It nearly went under her short red skirt. Lyzette froze.

"I would work long hours. I would be willing to do hard jobs," she stuttered, trying to ignore as his hand crept higher and nearly brushed her panties.

"How hard?" he said, taking her hand and putting it on his crotch.

She swallowed and stood up abruptly.

"I'm sorry, Mr. Loder, I think you've got me mixed up with some other sort of girl," she said, as firmly as she could manage. Her stomach was tied in knots. "I want a job as an assistant. Typing and answering phones."

"Oh, I'm sorry," he said. "I must have been mistaken. Have you seen the lovely view out the window?"

Lyzette felt taken aback and relieved at the sudden topic change. She would admire the view for hours if it meant Mr. Loder would keep his wandering hands off of her and his mind on her interview.

She walked over to the window and looked down on the city. If she weren't near-sighted, she would be able to see her house from here. She needed glasses, but she never wore them. Her mother said they made her look bookish and that she would never be a success if she appeared to be a nerd.

Her mother defined success as landing a man.

"It looks beautiful," she said.

"Something is certainly beautiful," Mr. Loder said. He stepped behind her, breathing into her ear and slipping his hands around her. He cupped her large breasts.

Lyzette spun around. It was a difficult feat in her tippy shoes.

"Mr. Loder, I think I had better go," she said, trying not to let her tears fall.

Mr. Loder frowned.

"Yes, you had better go before I have you thrown out. You come in here, dressed like that and you expect me to think that you want a job as an assistant? Women who look like you don't have respectable jobs, Lyzette. And if you're going to display your wares so openly, don't be surprised if a man might want to sample them."

He was angry, and Lyzette felt afraid. She left as quickly as she could. As she rode the elevator down the twenty-seven floors to ground level, she felt her hopes drop down into her fabulous shoes.

She wandered back out onto the sidewalk. She noticed that the man in the black suit was still hanging around on the street. He smiled at her again, like he knew something she didn't.

Maybe he wanted to feel her up like Mr. Loder. She took a shallow breath and darted past him, avoiding his eyes.

Had she done something wrong? Her mother had always told her to dress up when she wanted to leave a good impression on someone. That was all she had been doing. These were her nicest clothes. And she had wanted to impress Mr. Loder so that he would give her the job.

Now she had ruined it. He hadn't taken her seriously. He had implied that she was a whore and that she would drop her panties for anyone because she showed a bit of cleavage and leg.

She wasn't like that, and she wanted people to take her seriously.

As she stepped out into the street again and made her way down to the subway to go home, Lyzette realized she would never get a job as an assistant. She would have to go back to bartending because that was all she could do. At least there her cleavage got her good tips, and she could slap anyone who tried to feel her up.

But somehow, she knew that bartending wasn't enough. It would never be enough to satisfy her and make her feel like a success.

Her job wasn't enough.

Her life wasn't enough.

And neither was she.

* * *

Lyzette rode the subway in silence, staring at the dirty floor that was covered in gum wrappers, a flyer, the cap discarded from a bottle of juice, and the mud of thousands of shoes. When she got to her stop, she climbed the stairs with difficulty, wishing she could take off her ridiculous heels and be comfortable again. But she still had a twenty minute walk to get to her neighborhood.

She teetered along, trying not to get the spikes of her heels caught in any of the cracks in the sidewalk. She heard something behind her.

It made her nervous when she realized that someone was following her.

When she looked back and saw that it was the man in the black suit, she felt real fear.

Why was he trailing behind her? She walked faster, the clicking of her shoes echoing in the empty street. There weren't any shops or houses along this stretch. There was nowhere to duck into where there would be people who might help her. She kept on going and tried not to glance backwards. He didn't seem to be looking at her, but it was quite a coincidence that he went to her exact stop and then walked in the same direction that she was going in.

He must be a criminal that thought she was an easy target. And she knew now that he was right. She could have brought a sensible pair of shoes to walk in. She didn't have to wear the high heels all the way there — she could have put them on before she had gone into the interview. But no, she had to be stylish. Now she was paying the price.

She walked faster.

Lyzette reached her neighborhood and headed for home. She shuffled past the dingy houses and yards littered with trash, paying them no heed as she tried to reach her front door before the man caught up to her. When she got to the edge of her yard, she ran up the walk, not caring that she might break one of her heels off. She zipped up the stairs and threw open the door, slamming it behind her and locking it immediately.

"Lyz? Lyzzie? Is that you? Why are you slamming the door?" Her mother walked out of the kitchen. She wore a pantsuit in turquoise and make-up so thick it looked like a mask. Lyzette didn't pay her any attention as she crept to the living room window and peeked out around the faded drapes. "Lyzette. What is going on?"

"Shhh," she said, watching as the man in the black suit stopped and appeared to examine their neighbor's house. Then he looked back into their living room window as if he could see where she was hiding.

He smiled. He looked like he knew a private secret. Lyzette felt a little sick to her stomach.

"A man was following me home, Mama," she said, stepping back away from the window. "Should we call the cops?"

"Call the police?" her mother said, frowning. "What are you thinking? It's probably that overactive imagination of yours again, Lyzette. Anyone can see that he's a neighbor out for a stroll."

"Out for a stroll, Mama? Who can afford a suit like that and lives in our neighborhood?" she asked, looking at her mother like she was crazy. "And no one strolls around here. They might get shot!"

"Well, that's true. But he's probably visiting someone. You always think too highly of yourself, Lyzette," she said, scornfully. "And you're doing it again. He wasn't after you."

She stared at her mother. Had she been followed home by a deranged shadowy figure? Her mother thought she imagined it. It figured.

Not knowing what to do, Lyzette followed her routine. She pulled off her shoes and set them carefully in the closet, even though she wanted to throw them. She knew by now that would bring down her mother's wrath, and that was the last thing she needed. She placed the shoes side-by-side in the front closet and went into her room to change.

With precision, she pulled off her blouse and hung it neatly on the hanger. Then she unzipped her skirt and hung that correctly, too. She changed into comfortable cotton underwear and pulled on her favorite gray sweats and a T-shirt that said "I'm with Beautiful."

Her mother thought it was funny.

Then, as she always did when she needed comforting, she dropped on her bed and reached under the mattress, pulling out her sketch pad and pencil. Lyzette gave a happy little sigh and began to draw.

She quickly roughed in a jungle scene and added a woman that looked a bit like herself. She smiled, and her face got a thoughtful look as she turned the paper and made vivid strokes. After a minute, she held the pad away so she could see it better. She allowed herself a moment of satisfaction as she looked at the realistic scene of herself in a jungle, about to be eaten by a dangerous tiger.

Then her face fell as she thought about the man in the black suit. Would he come back? Was he waiting out there for her, right now? Closing her curtains made her feel better momentarily.

When she glanced at the drawing again, she felt a sense of foreboding, like she was a helpless female in a dangerous jungle with a tiger crouching and waiting to attack.

# CHAPTER 2

Lyzette stared at the dress in the shop window. She was sure the designer imagined a princess when she created it. It was gold and sparkled. The sleeves were puffed, with the skirt long enough to cover the feet of the lucky woman who got to wear it.

Lyzette thought that if she could have a dress like that just once in her life, she would be able to die happy. She wished she could have things like that. A princess dress, and a coffee maker that would make her favorite cappuccino every single morning that she wanted one.

Lyzette strolled on down the street, window shopping. She was worried that the man in the black suit would be waiting for her when she left today, but there hadn't been any sign of him. She was getting out of the house for an hour or two before she had to go to work.

It was her mother's day off. She tried her best to avoid her mother as much as possible on those days so she wouldn't bother her. It seemed to Lyzette that her mother thought her a nuisance and wished she would go away. Lyzette stayed out of her mother's vision by going out every Tuesday, looking through the windows on the street with the most expensive shops.

Lyzette wore a sundress that ended at her mid-thigh and had thin spaghetti straps. The dress was tight and hugged her round breasts together. If she wasn't careful and bent over, she might show someone her underwear. But she was always careful and always a lady. She did what her mother taught her and yet somehow things never worked out for her. She couldn't figure out what she was doing wrong. She thought she was doing everything correctly.

But if she was, what was the matter with her life?

She bought a newspaper once she was back in the regular part of town. Lyzette made sure she leaned forward, giving the man a good view of her breasts. The thin yellow material of the dress barely contained them. She smiled at him cheerfully and took her newspaper to the park. Her mother said it wasn't teasing — it was inspiring men to do what you wanted them to by using all of your assets.

On the front page was a story about yet another alien race. Her mother said that the President of Earth was trying to get everyone to like the weird aliens on other planets, but she was damned if she was going to. Her mother had preferred it when humans had thought they were the only ones in the galaxy.

Lyzette ignored the stories about aliens. She didn't care about that sort of thing, and instead she turned to the comics page and read all her favorites, laughing aloud at some of the silly ones. She surprised herself by finishing the entire word search.

The newspaper took her full attention. If she had been more aware of her surroundings, she would have noticed men consistently giving her looks that would make her blush. They had been doing that since she was fourteen and started needing a bra.

The looks were nearly always at her chest and not her face. Her mother said that men were only after one thing, and there wasn't a decent one that roamed the Earth. The only thing to do was to catch one and make him give you everything you wanted. That was the ticket to a fabulous lifestyle.

Lyzette didn't imagine all men could be dangerous. Some had been kind to her. Old Eddie at the pawn shop was sweet when she brought in her mother's jewelry to sell.

She couldn't think of any others, but that didn't mean there weren't any.

When she got on the crowded five o'clock bus back to her neighborhood, there weren't any seats available. She was forced to stand and hold onto the overhead straps. This made her uncomfortable because her dress rode up high, and her breasts pushed out too much. The men on the bus either glanced at her when they thought she wasn't looking, or openly leered at her. One guy got on a few stops after her and grabbed the strap beside her. He swayed his body into hers every time the bus driver braked.

Lyzette was red-faced and embarrassed by the time she got off the bus. She was two streets away from her house. It was late, and the sun had already gone down. She felt anxious. She should have caught the earlier bus, but she had wanted to stay out as long as possible and enjoy being out.

She realized it had been a stupid decision. It was dark enough to obscure her vision but not shadowy enough for the street lights to activate. She pulled her skirt down yet again and made her way home. At least she was only wearing chunky one-inch heels.

She made sure to walk down a different street today than the one she took yesterday when the man in the black suit had followed her.

This street was well-lit, which made her feel better. There was only a one-block stretch where there was complete darkness and she would walk quickly across that part. She would be home in five minutes and her mother could tell her again that she had been imagining things.

But instead of going straight home, on a whim she stopped at the local bar to pick up some fries and a sandwich for dinner. Her mother didn't cook on her day off, and she didn't feel like having macaroni and cheese tonight.

The bar was crowded inside. There were three or four tables that were full. One of the tables had a bunch of young, drunk guys.

She placed her order and waited by the cash register. One of the young men sidled up to her and stood close enough to make her feel uncomfortable.

"Hey," he said. "How are you?"

"I'm fine, thank you," she said. Lyzette wished she had stopped at the deli instead.

She didn't ask him to step back. In her experience, they never did.

"Want to have a beer at our table?" he said, smiling charmingly.

"No thank you. I need to get home."

"I could take you home," he said, stepping back and looking her up and down. When he finished examining her body, he licked his lips.

Lyzette swallowed. God, she hated this. Why did it keep happening to her?

"No, thank you. I'll be fine."

"Well, see you around then," he said. He went back to his table, but she could feel his eyes undressing her as she stood.

Finally, her order came, and she took the two bags and pushed the door open with her back. Lyzette headed down the street, and to her dismay she noticed that the man who had approached her in the pub was leaving and walking down the sidewalk behind her. Darn it.

She wasn't being followed again, was she? Twice in two days was too much. She needed to call the cops. But she didn't want to stop now because she thought that might be dangerous too, so she kept on walking.

Soon she got to the block where there was poor illumination. She noticed that there was a dark alley halfway up the street. Lyzette wondered how she could have forgotten about that alleyway. Her breathing sped up as she felt fear squeeze her heart. She glanced back and saw that the young man had nearly closed the distance between them. She accelerated and felt her calves and quads burning as she walked as fast as she could.

But it was no use. By the time she was almost at the alley, he was beside her.

"Hey there," he said. "Can I carry one of those bags for you, beautiful?"

"No thank you," Lyzette said, looking straight ahead. "I'm fine."

"You are fine," he said. "Damn fine."

He stepped in front of her and forced her to stop. She could see her bosom heaving from her fast breathing, and she knew he had noticed it too.

"Are you out of breath or turned on?" he asked. "A slut like you probably likes it in alleyways, huh?"

He grabbed her arm and began to walk her into the darkness. Lyzette struggled, but it was too late. He

19

dragged her along. Soon she could make out what was in the alleyway: a dumpster for trash and a doorway with two steps going up to it.

He pressed his body towards her and backed her up against the wall. Her bags of food were dropped and forgotten on the dark, dirty, pavement of the alley. She realized at that moment that she was in big trouble.

She was alone with a man who clearly only wanted one thing — her jewel. And he would take it if she wouldn't give it to him. There was no one to help her because her mother didn't know where she was. Anyone from the pub would want a turn instead of helping her.

She felt his hard chest pressing against her soft mounds as he pinned her to the wall. She took a breath to scream and found her mouth covered by his as he kissed her forcefully. He tasted like beer. His demanding tongue thrust into her mouth, and his hands palmed her breasts, squeezing and pinching her nipples.

She made an unhappy sound and struggled, but her resistance only seemed to inflame him more. He lifted her up and wrapped her legs around his waist. She felt something hard pushing against her panties.

That was his cock, she knew, which would push up inside her taking her jewel. She had to get out of this situation immediately.

He pulled his head away from hers to rip her dress down, allowing her breasts to spill out of the tiny bra that held them in check. He groaned and bent to take one in his mouth, and as his face came down, Lyzette drew her head back and walloped him on the nose with her forehead.

"Ow!" he yelled, dropping her and putting his hands on his face. Blood poured out.

Lyzette scrambled to her feet. The man's blood was all over her beautiful dress. She ran for the opening of the alley as fast as she could go, and kicked off her shoes so she could run faster.

"Get back here, you fucking whore," the man growled behind her, but Lyzette didn't stop. Just then, she looked up and saw his friends from the bar closing off her escape.

Lyzette knew that worse things than losing her jewel were in store if they trapped her in the alley. She knew what happened to girls that were caught by a bunch of guys who only wanted one thing.

She skidded to a stop and searched for some other means of escape. She would take any help. At that moment, the door leading into the alley opened, spilling a sharp slice of light into the darkness.

It was as if heaven itself was opening up for her.

"Hey," a voice said. "Do you need help?"
"Yes," she nearly sobbed.

"Come in here. Come on, quick," the voice said.

And Lyzette gratefully scrambled through the door. As it shut behind her, she heard the men pounding on it and yelling.

"Oh my God," she said. "Thank you."

She looked around to see who it was that had saved her and noticed she was in an empty room that echoed with the sounds of her shaky voice. There was a bare light bulb with a grimy string hanging from it.

"It was my pleasure," said the voice. She realized it had a grating edge that made her instantly nervous. When she moved to the sound, she saw that it belonged to someone with their back to her. But even before he turned around, she recognized the black suit.

"What...what...?" she stammered. Out of the frying pan and into the fire, she thought.

"Don't worry," he said. "I won't fuck you like they would have, much as I would like to. My employers frown on such behavior, but that doesn't mean I can't copy a feel ever now and then," he said. He reached out to fondle her breasts, which she realized were still hanging out of her dress. She hadn't had time to stuff them back in.

"Who do you work for?" she asked.

He laughed. "I guess it doesn't matter now," he said. "You know the mail-order bride company that has all the commercials? TerraMates?"

Lyzette nodded numbly. Their advertising was everywhere, and it looked like a fun adventure. She might have signed up herself, but she wasn't sure about getting married to an alien.

"Sometimes they don't get enough volunteers, and hire independent contractors to increase their bridal pool. Some might call it abduction, or stealing girls off the streets. I prefer to think of it as gainful employment. I mean, I work hard selecting the appropriate candidates." He looked at Lyzette's body appreciatively. "Don't worry. You'll be well taken care of, and they will generously compensate me."

Somehow that didn't make Lyzette feel any better. She stood still, allowing him to touch her because she had a feeling this man was far more dangerous than the ones on the other side of the door. She felt like an animal on the highway at night, transfixed by the lights.

"Nice." He bent down to suck her nipple into his mouth. She shuddered. She was more afraid than she had ever been in her life.

Without warning, he bit her sharply, and she cried out. In seconds, her knees buckled and her vision got blurry. But before she went completely unconscious, she saw that his eyes had a hint of yellow.

Was he human?

# CHAPTER 3

When she came to, Lyzette looked around fearfully for her captor, but there was no one in sight. She was in another empty room. This one had indirect lighting and she couldn't see where the light was coming from.

Blood covered her dress. It was from the man she had head-butted. Her dress was now ripped and torn in several places, revealing more of her skin than she would like. She checked herself over to see if anyone or anything had molested her, but her pride and purity both seemed intact.

Her arms and legs were bruised and scraped. Perhaps she had been tossed around. It seemed unusual that her lady parts were unharmed. As she checked herself over, she thought about the strange not-man that had bitten her breast.

He was clearly an alien.

Unlike many people on Earth, she had no problems with aliens in general. But she didn't like them specifically biting her and knocking her out.

She had watched a few documentaries on some of the other species that inhabited the galaxy, and she had never heard of one that had greenish skin, yellow eyes, and a venomous bite. Apparently she needed to watch a few more.

She pulled her dress down and found that she had teeth marks on her skin. The wound was turning a strange green color, and she hoped that it wasn't getting infected. By the look of it, the cuts had healed a significant amount, and Lyzette immediately wondered how long she had been asleep.

She stood up, tucking her breasts back in and pulling down her dress by habit. She walked across the room. Smooth plastic covered the walls, and there was no door. The floor ran up into the walls seamlessly.

She might as well have been in a box, not a room.

She frowned, sitting down on the floor again. She felt woozy when she stood up. After an hour or two, she felt tired, and she lay down to sleep.

* * *

When Lyzette awoke the second time, she felt the urge to urinate. She called out and waited to see if anyone would answer.

No one did. She didn't know if that was good or bad.

She decided to hold it as long as she could before she polluted the corner. She knew her room would start to smell once she had to go, and she would put it off as long as possible.

She wondered if anyone would attend to her or if she was supposed to stay here until she died. She had no way of knowing how long she had been in there and no way of tracking time. She didn't have a watch, and there were no windows.

After another hour of being awake, she couldn't control her bladder any longer, and she relieved herself in a corner. At least she wasn't drinking, she thought; she wouldn't have to do this again any time soon. Her stomach rumbled. She realized it had been a very long time since her last meal.

She stared at the walls and wondered what her mother was doing since she had disappeared. Mom certainly wasn't calling the police to report her missing. Lyzette thought longingly about the club sandwich and fries that were rotting in the alley.

She would give anything for a bite of a sandwich right now — even her jewel.

After another few hours, she started feeling sleepy again and wondered why she couldn't stay awake. She lay down, drifting off immediately.

---

When Lyzette awoke for the third time, things had changed.

She was in a different room. She was on a bed; it was not a comfortable bed, but a bed nonetheless. Her dress was gone, and she was wearing an outfit that made her even less comfortable. Especially when she thought about how it had to get on her body.

It was similar to a swimsuit, but most of the suit was missing. Cups covered and supported her breasts like a push-up bra. She wore tiny panties that narrowed to a thong in the back, and her butt was hanging out. Several strips of fabric went across her midsection in an X shape but didn't cover anything. Two more straps crossed her back and attached to her panties.

She felt completely exposed.

There was a thin blanket on the bed, and she wrapped it around herself like a towel, covering her body. With nothing else to do, she sat down on the bed to wait.

Somehow her bladder was full again. That's when she noticed that there was a screened-off area of the room, and when she went behind it, there was a toilet and a tiny sink. These were the luxury suites in an alien spaceship hotel.

She used the bathroom and washed up. Once she was finished with her short cleaning routine, though, she got restless and returned to the bed.

Apparently she was dressed this way and in this room for a reason. She had only to wait and see what it was.

Lyzette wasn't sure when it happened. It was impossible to tell time. She could have been there for minutes, hours, or days. All she knew was that after she blinked, there was someone in the room with her.

It was the man in the black suit.

He looked exactly the same as before. He wasn't wearing panties or a weird alien outfit. She instinctively pressed herself against the wall and pulled the blanket around her more tightly. Her bite wounds throbbed as he smiled at her.

"Are you ready, little human?" he said.

"Ready for what?" Lyzette squeaked. She hated how small her voice sounded.

"You're going to be on display. There'll be no modesty allowed, unfortunately. Covering yourself with a blanket is simply out of the question when I take you out there. Remember that."

"When you take me out where?" Her heart started to pound. What was going on? She felt completely lost and at the mercy of this creature.

He didn't explain.

"There are going to be a lot of people interested in you. And you are going to smile and look pretty so that one of them will choose you. Do you understand? I want you to be selected this round, and if you don't, then I will be very displeased. You don't want to see me upset."

She certainly didn't. His eyes bored into hers, and she wished he would look away. He walked over to her and pulled her roughly to her feet. She lost her hold on the blanket, and it fell to the floor. He smiled when he saw her nearly naked body.

"I didn't fuck you because I want someone to choose you. You're most valuable if you're pure. But if you don't go, all bets are off. And I will split you in two, little human. Mordeelans are well endowed, very well endowed."

Lyzette felt her eyes grow wide as she watched him adjust what looked like a snake in his pants. She knew he meant that he would take her jewel.

She didn't know what he meant when he said he would split her in two, but it sounded terribly unpleasant.

"I almost hope you don't go," he whispered in her ear, squeezing one of her butt cheeks.

She didn't have a clue what he was talking about, but she would smile, and she would look cute.

She would do anything to get away from him.

---

Once she was in the cage, she thought perhaps there were some things she would not do to get away from him.

Aliens tied her up with her arms and legs spread-eagled. The thong left little to any alien's imagination. She had been tied so that her back was arched. Her breasts bulged and nearly tumbled out of their confinement.

After the first three hours, she had stopped blushing.

When the sixteenth alien male had reached in through the bars to squeeze her breasts or slide his hand between her cheeks, she stopped noticing the deep feeling of shame that filled her.

She knew now where she was. It was a slave market, and she was for sale.

Her abductor tied her up and left her hanging in the cage, chatting up potential buyers from a distance. She couldn't hear what was said, and she didn't care. All she wanted was for someone to buy her so she could get out of this painful, humiliating position and sit down.

A large, muscular male with a tail came by and smiled at her. She didn't like how any of them smiled, but she particularly didn't like the way this one was looking at her — like she was a piece of meat.

He came up to the cage and his tail slid through the bars. He met her eyes while he slipped his tail between her legs, rubbing her lady parts. She tried not to flinch away because she had learned that made them even more eager. She could barely stand him touching her.

"How much?" he shouted to the Mordeelan.

"Would you like to come over here and discuss a price?"

"No. I want to keep touching the whore with my tail while you tell me the price, you fucking idiot."

Her captor named an impossibly large number of credits, nearly making Lyzette choke. She couldn't be worth that much money. As her potential new owner retrieved the funds, she watched another humanoid male walk up to her cage.

"Done." The alien man who had captured her was practically dancing a jig, he was so happy.

"How much for this female?" the new alien said. He ignored the fact that the negotiation was complete.

"I'm sorry, I just sold her."

"She's my property now."

The new alien flipped his arm over, pulling back his shirt to show three purple interlocking circles on the inside of his forearm. It reminded Lyzette of Venn diagrams she had made in math class a thousand light-years ago, back home on Earth.

She was surprised to see both males back off. Her purchaser lifted his hands, palms facing out.

"She's yours if you want, buddy. No hard feelings."

"I'm not your buddy," the new male said. He wasn't smiling.

"Of course not. Of course not. I'll be going now," he said, backing away with his tail between his legs.

Lyzette would have laughed if she hadn't been in such a horrible situation. The tattoo terrified them.

"How much?"

"Whatever you want to pay, Markanor," her captor said, squatting and placing his hand, palm out, on his forehead. Lyzette assumed it was a gesture of respect.

The male named a price that was half of what the other man had agreed to pay. Her abductor seemed to wilt but didn't comment.

"Thank you, sir," was all he said.

Lyzette was trembling with panic by the time she was untied and taken out of the cage. The Markanor never even looked at her. What would he do to her? Where were they going? And who was he that he could command that much respect and fear?

She followed him out of the slave market, walking as fast as she could in her bare feet. He was tall and had broad shoulders. He was the kind of guy who worked out a lot. He had a square jaw. She had noticed that his eyes were blue. They seemed cold and maybe cruel.

He swiped his arm over a scanner, which allowed them to pass through a door. On the other side was what looked like an empty mall. Everything was closed. He pointed at a bench.

"Sit," he said, curtly.
Did he think she was a dog?

But she sat because her legs could barely hold her up anymore.

He walked over to a ladies clothing store and swiped his arm over the lock. It opened, and he passed in. Lyzette watched in confusion as he grabbed clothes from the racks, swiping his arm again over the payment scanners. He locked the store again and came over to her.

"Here," he said, still not meeting her eyes. "Put these on. You look like a whore."

"Aren't I?" she wanted to ask but didn't dare to. Maybe she wasn't a whore. She certainly hoped not. But she didn't have much hope.

Everyone she had seen so far only wanted to take her jewel, and she had a hard time believing that he would be any different. Her new master was a dominant alpha, and she would do well to keep him pleased.

He didn't turn around, so she turned her back to him to give herself a modicum of privacy as she put on her new outfit.

"I didn't tell you to move, I told you to change your clothes," he said coldly.

She clenched her teeth together and turned back towards him. She stripped off the weird outfit she was wearing and quickly donned the new panties, bra, and dress.

She felt a tiny bit better immediately.

"Let's go," he said. Because he had shown her a small kindness, she felt bold enough to ask a question.

"Where are we going?"

He turned and met her eyes for the first time. All she saw there was emptiness.

"I will brand you," he said matter-of-factly.

Did he realize he was saying that he was going to burn Lyzette's skin to show his ownership of her as if she were no more than a prize heifer? Her stomach curled into a cold ball of dread. When would this madness end?

"As long as people know you are mine, you will not be harmed."

Perhaps to an alien, burning her on purpose with a hot iron was not harming her. He turned and walked down the hallway, not bothering to see if she followed him.

He knew she had no choice.

# CHAPTER 4

Lyzette awoke to the sound of birds singing. She opened her eyes. Her muscles were sore, and she was confused. Where was she and what was going on? She wasn't in her shabby little bedroom.

The room was white, all white, with a royal blue accent here and there — the button on a pillow, a ribbon, a picture with three blue interlocking circles.

In shock, she remembered everything that had happened. The attack on Earth and being saved by the alien man who kidnapped her. Stuck in a cage and trussed up like an animal. And the tail alien nearly buying her before the man called the Markanor had changed everything — waving his forearm around and scaring everyone.

He seemed kind when he had given her clothes and provided her with a bed to rest on during their shuttle flight down to the planet. But when she tried to thank him, she was informed that the Markanors always treated their slaves well.

He put her in her place, in case she was getting the idea that she was not a slave.

Still, the room was fantastic.

It was large and airy, with windows on three of the walls. She realized sunlight was coming in through two of the windows, even though they were on opposite sides.

There were sheer white curtains that blew softly with the breeze, reminding her of fancy houses in the Caribbean.

The bed was large and had a white canopy with several layers of blankets and a pile of fluffy pillows. There was a breakfast table with two chairs in one corner, and a desk and armchair along the other wall. The wooden door was stained dark brown. Lyzette had no idea if there were trees on the planet. She didn't even know the name of this world. She would not have recognized the name of the planet, even if anyone had thought to tell her.

Lyzette got up and looked around. It turned out that one window was a set of French doors that opened onto a balcony. The balcony contained a small table and two chairs. On the table was a simple meal, accompanied by a cup of steaming hot liquid. She wondered if it was for her and realized that she didn't care.

She was ravenous.

It had been at least two days since she had eaten, and she was starving. She gobbled everything and wished there was more.

"It's not good to eat too much right away," a voice said behind her. She spun around on her chair, feeling wary.

She saw a woman with long braided hair that hung down her back. She walked out of the room and onto the balcony, leaning against the railing.

"The Mordeelans have venom that knocks their victims out but has some strange side effects, not the least of which is an upset stomach. As far as we can tell, you were sedated about a week ago. You're still getting the poison out of your system," the woman said.

"A week?" Lyzette said. It was unbelievable.

"Yes, it takes five days to get from Earth to Marka, plus a day at the slave market. Close enough to a week," she said, shrugging.

"Any other side effects?" Lyzette asked, suddenly worried now that she knew she wasn't going to die immediately.

"The male Mordeelans have overactive libidos. Their bite makes mating more pleasurable for the female so that the male can get more sex."

Lyzette wrinkled her nose. She felt disgusted.

"Still, that will help," the blonde woman said, coming and sitting down at the table. Lyzette eyed her suspiciously.

"Help with what?"

"Your first time," she said. "My name is Raimey."

"Lyzette."

"Nice to meet you," the woman said.

"I wish I could say the same about you, but I'm not sure yet," Lyzette said honestly.

"I don't blame you for being distrustful," Raimey said. "It's probably a good thing. But for what it's worth, you can trust me."

"Why should I?"

"Because I've been in your position before. I know the feelings you're experiencing. I can help you make the most out of your situation."

"What do you mean? Help me do what?"

"To get the Markanor to take you as his wife. It's what all the slaves hope for, but none has ever seen it happen."

Raimey explained to Lyzette that every few years, the Markanor went and purchased a new consort from the slave market. He never got emotionally involved with the women at all. They were simply a means of relieving the sexual pressure that built up every couple days in a Markan's body.

"They desire to have sex all the time. Their society prevents them from taking more than one mate at a time, so they need to find a woman who can handle having sex very, very frequently. The Markanor doesn't care if his slave can handle it or not. He fucks her whenever he wants because she's his property."

"That sounds barbaric," Lyzette said, feeling afraid again.

"Don't start thinking that he's an asshole. He isn't. And he's a good lover," Raimey assured me.

"How do you know?" Lyzette said, frowning.

"Because I used to be his consort, until he cast me aside for the next new thing. Now, I'm a house slave."

"Oh," Lyzette said, taken aback at Raimey's revelation. "Is that my future?"

"I know how to get him to take you as his wife."

"Why would you want to help me?" Lyzette said, still feeling suspicious.

"Because it would be a victory for all the slaves if one of us elevated to the position of mistress of the house."

"What kind of victory?" Surely that couldn't be all she would gain when she got married?

"The mistress can give the slaves their freedom by sending them off the planet," she said. "We keep thinking that if only the Markanor would marry one of the slaves, then she could free us all. Every one of us has tried. But none of us have succeeded."

Lyzette stared at Raimey. That was quite a burden.

"How many slaves are there?"

"Seven of us now, including you," Raimey said, matter-of-factly.

Lyzette had never taken care of anyone besides herself. Her mother had not even trusted her enough to let her babysit the next door neighbor's children. Did Raimey want her to take responsibility for the lives of six people?

She was a no one from Earth. Just some slave now. The flavor of the month for an alien male who was going to use her up and spit her out. She couldn't do what Raimey said. She couldn't save all those people. The Markanor was ruthless and took what he wanted. She had no power to make him care for her enough to want to marry her.

What was this woman thinking?

"Just consider it, okay?" Raimey said, getting up.

Lyzette nodded, feeling overwhelmed. The day had just begun.

"Come on. We've got to prepare you."

"For what?" she asked.

"For your first time, silly," Raimey said. "Your bath is all ready, and then we must begin the training."

"The training?" Her voice trembled. "In what?"

"In making love, of course," Raimey said. "You must please the Markanor. It is crucial."

41

\* \* \*

She knew the other women were watching. With her eyes shut tightly, Lyzette had been able to ignore them all. She lay panting and sweaty on the bed with her hand still up under her nightgown.

She couldn't even speak as the spasms shook her body.

"That's what you are looking for when he takes you the first time," Raimey told her. Lyzette had washed and was sitting in the circle of women on her bed. "The Markanors take pride in making their females come every time. It is a great dishonor if the male was to come before the female, so it is good that you are so orgasmic, Lyzette."

"I'm orgasmic?" she said, faintly.

"How long, Maureen?" Raimey asked an older woman.

"Four minutes, twenty-five seconds."

"You can come quickly. If you can come that fast when he's inside you, you've got it made."

Lyzette stared at the women. She was pretty sure that if he stuck his big thing up inside her, she'd be screaming in pain, not in pleasure the way she just had. She didn't believe having the Markanor up inside her was going to feel good. It simply wasn't possible. But she knew that the women were counting on her, and she nodded.

It felt like an enormous burden that she had never asked for, but even so Lyzette felt something inside herself that she had never felt before. If she had to guess what it was, she would say it was strength. But she had never had any self-confidence or belief in herself, so she didn't know what it felt like.

Still, she liked it.

"Listen, Lyzette. You never know when he will call for you, so you have to be prepared. The most important thing to know is that he likes to be in control."

Lyzette nodded again. As if she would be taking control. What a laugh, she thought.

"And never shave down there," a red-headed woman said. "He likes his women natural. He says he isn't a pervert, and he doesn't want a damn child."

"And whatever you do, don't get on top unless he asks you to," a black woman said, shuddering. "He spanked me so hard I couldn't stand up for days."

Lyzette swallowed hard. Spanking?

"Don't worry, Lyzette. He doesn't usually do that. Delia is the only one of us that he has ever spanked for doing something wrong in bed. And don't pretend that you don't like it because you know you did. Stop scaring her, Delia. She's worried enough as it is."

Raimey frowned at Delia, who immediately snapped her mouth closed.

"When you get the call, it's a good idea to touch yourself beforehand so you're ready when it's time. You have an hour in his chambers before he comes in. You can spend some of that time getting yourself prepped," another woman said.

"Yeah, that's a good plan," someone else agreed.

"Why?" Lyzette said, confused.

"Well, it's like this, Lyz," Maureen said. "Women and men are both climbing hills when they're making love. It's just that the man takes about ten minutes to get to the top, but it takes a woman at least half an hour. Typical women, not like you."

"Climbing hills?" Lyzette said, feeling confused.

"Yes, and the men climb faster than the women. If you get started climbing your hill before you get near him, then you have a shorter distance to go, and you have a better chance of finishing at the same time."

"Oh," Lyzette said. She wondered what the hell they meant.

"It's giving the slower person in a race a head start, that way the faster person and the more deliberate person finish together. That's the idea," Raimey said, and all the women laughed.

Lyzette felt out of her depth. How would she remember all their advice?

How was she supposed to relax and have an orgasm if she was so worried about screwing up and ruining their plans? And what would happen when he took her jewel?

Lyzette found herself hyperventilating a little at the thought. She also felt sad. She wanted to give her jewel to her husband. The man she would love.

Now she had to give it to an alien because she was a slave on a foreign planet.

It wasn't fair, but it was her new life. She would have to make the best of it. All she had to do was wait to be called by the Markanor.

# CHAPTER 5

Three days later, she was still waiting.

It was breakfast time. "He'll call you soon, Lyzzie, don't worry," Maureen said, patting her knee.

Lyzette certainly hoped so. Or did she? She didn't know what she wanted. She only knew that waiting was making her crazy. She felt like she needed something badly, but she didn't know what it was. She was going to explode if she didn't get whatever it was soon.

The women said it was natural to be feeling that way. When the Markanor first acquired them, everyone had a similar reaction. Lyzette didn't understand half of what they were saying, but she smiled and nodded and tried to do as they asked. In this strange new world, she was attempting to keep her head above water, and once she got used to things, maybe she would figure everything out.

Her summons came in the afternoon. Lyzette thought it odd that he didn't wait until the evening.

"Lyz, the Markanor wants sex when the Markanor wants sex. Your job is to show up, enjoy it, and please him," said Raimey.

"Besides, it'll last well into the night, won't it girls?" Maureen said.

Lyzette had a hard time believing that Maureen had been his consort once, but the women said it was true. They wouldn't lie to her, would they?

"Come on Lyzzie, let's get you all ready," Raimey said. They had been sitting at a table shelling peas, but everyone stopped what they were doing when the summons came.

Raimey took her to the bathhouse. Lyzette washed everywhere. She was provided pleasant smelling oils to rub all over her body — even in her private parts.

"Don't put too much of the tangerine oil down there," Raimey cautioned her. "He doesn't like the taste."

Lyzette stared at her, frozen in place.

"What is he going to be tasting down there?" she asked weakly.

Raimey laughed and handed her a handful of white cloth.

"Here, put this on. It's lingerie. Then I'll do your hair a little."

Lyzette pulled on panties and stockings that came up to her thigh. The top was a tiny dress that was so short that it showed some of her underwear. A bra in the little dress shoved her breasts up into cleavage. Raimey finished by handing her a pair of matching high heels, which Lyzette put on eagerly.

"Turn around."

Lyzette spun in a slow circle.

"Wow, you look great. He likes his women to *look* innocent, but you *are* innocent. Won't he be surprised?" Raimey murmured.

She stepped in front of the mirror without answering Raimey and stared at herself. She was a vision in white. Her dark brown hair was long, loose, and curling. Her curvy body looked good, with the lingerie emphasizing all her best parts and minimizing the bad.

"You'd better get over there," Raimey said. "You don't want to be late."

Lyzette nodded mutely and headed for the door.

"Hey, Lyzzie," Raimey said, and Lyzette turned around. "He won't hurt you, you know. You don't have anything to worry about."

Lyzette doubted that was true, but she tried to smile to show she wasn't afraid.

She didn't convince Raimey.

"Do you want me to walk you over?" Raimey offered.

"No, I'm fine, Raimey. Thank you for all your help," Lyzette said formally. Then she went out the door.

When she arrived at his room, she knocked timidly.

"Come in," she heard his rough, deep voice say.

She couldn't move.

This was really happening. His voice on the other side of the door proved it. And she wasn't ready. She didn't want this. She refused to give her jewel to him.

"Come in," the gravelly voice repeated, sounding a little more irritated this time.

She could run. She could escape. She could change clothes and leave. No one would stop her.

Or maybe they would.

Everyone knew he was taking her for the first time today. And they all knew she was nervous about it. And what about the women that had their hopes of freedom pinned on her?

Lyzette felt the weight of responsibility descend on her shoulders. She felt as if she were suffocating. Everyone was forcing her into doing something. She had never had to take care of anyone other than herself. Her mother had never expected Lyzette's help. But now everything was different. Now all these people were counting on her to go through with this and make the Markanor happy.

Lyzette felt a big ball of dread in the pit of her stomach, but she squared her shoulders, stood up tall, and put her hand on the doorknob.

At that moment, the door flew open, startling her so that she stumbled backward.

"What are you doing out there?" the Markanor said, apparently angry with her. "I called you to come in, twice."

He held up two strong fingers in front of her face.

Lyzette was afraid and couldn't answer. She stood in silence, staring at him with big eyes. He looked at her a moment and then stepped back, tilting his head to the side as if examining her.

"What's wrong?" he said, gruffly.

Lyzette still felt paralyzed. She couldn't do this.

"Why are you looking at me like that?" he said. "Like you're afraid."

Lyzette swallowed.

"Answer me, damn it," he said, getting angry again.

Her eyes got wide, and she became fearful. She managed to say something and answer him.

"Because I am afraid," she whispered. It was all she could manage.

He looked taken aback and dismayed.

"Why are you scared? None of the others were afraid," he told her.

"Maybe none of them showed they were," Lyzette suggested, her voice still barely above a whisper. She had her arms crossed over her chest and held her body back away from the Markanor. His height was intimidating, even though she was wearing heels. His hulking form scared her more than his anger. She wondered how she would endure this trial.

He frowned down at her.

"You're different. I don't know if I like it," he said, leaning back against the door frame and studying her. "I hope I don't have to get a refund. The Mordeelan looked like he wanted to have a lot of fun with you if he ended up keeping you."

Lyzette felt a lump come into her throat. She wasn't the smartest tool in the shed, but she knew a kind master when she saw one. She certainly didn't want to go back to the Mordeelan with the snake in his pants who had captured her. He would be much worse than the Markanor.

She had to pull herself together before he decided he didn't want her.

"I'm sorry for being different," she said, in a slightly louder voice. "I'll try not to be."

He stared at her for a moment and then burst out laughing.

"You are a strange little human, aren't you?" he said.

"I guess. Can I come in now?"

"Certainly, certainly," he said, stepping to the side and allowing Lyzette to scurry past him into his room.

She didn't notice his eyes take in every inch of her as she went past. When she turned around and faced him, ready to endure whatever he would do to her, she saw that his pants were bulging.

Shit. Inside his pants was his thing that he would put in her. She shivered a little in fear but picked up her chin and looked him in the eye.

"I'm ready now. I'm sorry I wasn't when I arrived. You may do with me as you wish," she told him, bravely.

He stared at her. Lyzette was a bizarre puzzle that he couldn't figure out.

"Of course I may. I'm your master."

"Right," she said, blushing deeply. Who was she to tell him what he could and couldn't do?

"Thank you for your permission," he said. "I have to say that I'm at a loss for how to proceed. I've never taken a woman who was afraid of me." Lyzette lifted her head. "That I knew was scared of me," he amended. "And I'm not sure I want to start now."

"Does it remind you of slavery?" Lyzette said, then slapped her hand over her mouth with a smacking sound. Why had she said that?

He looked at her as if he were seeing her for the first time.

"Yes, I suppose that is what it reminds me of," he said, studying her with a confused face.

She didn't point out again that she was his slave, and he could take her if he wanted to because she belonged to him — fear or no fear. He had paid for her.

Then the Markanor turned and looked out the window.

"You may go now," he said.

"Go?" Lyzette repeated. Was this a strange alien expression that she didn't understand? Did it mean that she should undress?

"Yes, go. Back to your room."

"Back to my room?" she frowned. "No. I'm not afraid. I swear. I don't want to go back to my room."

She could not have failed already. All she had to do was lie there and let him put his cock inside of her, and she had somehow screwed it up already? It wasn't possible. She had to do this. She made herself walk across the room and reached out and tentatively touched his hand.

"I want..." she hesitated, not sure what to say to convince him to desire her again.

"What?" he said, turning to her. His blue eyes that had been cold now blazed with heat. "What do you want?"

"I want you to take me to bed," she said firmly.

"Are you sure of that? I've never raped a woman, and I don't intend to start now. I have an abundance of females falling over themselves to be with me. I don't need a reluctant one."

"I'm sure," she said, nodding her head decisively.

"You say that like you've made up your mind to do something unpleasant, and you're getting ready to grin and bear it."

What could she do? Congratulate him on his remarkable powers of perception?

"No. I will not have a consort who is unwilling. Go and change into regular clothes — pants, not a dress — and meet me in the stables in half an hour."

"What? No. I swear. I'll do whatever you want. Don't send me back."

Everyone was counting on her and here she was fucking everything up again, as usual. Tears filled Lyzette's eyes, but she didn't let them fall, trying to hold it together.

"I'm not sending you back. I'm taking you on an excursion. Stop that crying. I can't stand it when women cry," he said, scowling at her.

"An excursion," she said, wiping away the tears. He wasn't going to give her back to the Mordeelan. She felt a surge of relief. "You're not firing me?"

He laughed again.

"A slave cannot be fired," he said. "Get dressed. No, wait. Show me your forearm."

Lyzette flipped her left forearm over and showed him the three interlocking circles. It hadn't hurt because they had given her local anesthesia, and it had only taken a second.

He bared his forearm and pressed his circles over hers. The moment their skin touched, she felt a jolt of excitement go from her belly to her sex.

"Okay, that's all I needed," he said. His breathing was not steady. His muscular chest rose and fell. "You can go."

Lyzette dashed into the hallway. She pulled off her heels and when she was a few doors away, she ran back to her room in her bare feet. She could hardly believe her luck. He wasn't going to take her jewel right now, and it seemed she hadn't messed everything up.

It was too good to be true.

"Why are you back already?" Raimey said. There was worry in her eyes when she saw Lyzette. "Are you okay? Did something go wrong?"

"I was afraid, and he knew it," she said, biting her lip. "He said he'd never raped a woman before, and he wasn't going to start now. He told me to get dressed and meet him at the stables."

Lyzette went to her closet and started pulling random clothes out. Women were coming in from the common room, the kitchen, and the other rooms as word spread that she had returned already.

"He didn't fuck you?" the redhead said.

"He said he wouldn't rape her," someone said.

"And he's taking her riding? That doesn't make sense."

The women's voices babbled on while Lyzette tried on outfit after outfit, not liking any of them.

"Wait," Raimey's voice cut through the crowd. "He didn't touch you at all, Lyz?"

Lyzette pulled on a pale pink crop top over her bra and drew her eyebrows together, trying to remember.

"No, he did touch me. He stopped me and asked to see my brand." She flipped over her forearm as she had done before.

"And he pressed his arm against mine."

"And…?" Raimey and the others leaned in. Their eyes were interested. Some of them bit their lips like they couldn't wait to hear the end of the story. "Did you feel anything?"

Lyzette dropped her eyes, feeling her whole face turning beet red at the thought of what she had felt.

"Ooooh, she did!" Delia squealed.

"What? What's so important?" Lyzette asked, but Raimey interrupted her.

"It's the challenge of courtship," she said, almost jumping up and down in her excitement. "Among Markans, when the male wants to court someone, he will press his arm to hers. It's a signal that he is interested in her as a mate and that he will be pursuing her."

"He's going to try to win you, Lyzette."

"But he doesn't have to win me. I'm his slave."

"He doesn't have to. But he's issued the challenge, which means he wants to win your heart. He wants you to want him. And a Markan, once he has issued the challenge, would never take a woman unwillingly. You won't be having sex with him unless you ask. He won't even touch you unless you beg him to take you."

Lyzette looked at Raimey. She would never beg him to do that. So it seemed she was safe. He would have to find another consort, and she would be a house slave. She was sure some of these more experienced women would be much better than she would.

But she wouldn't think about it right now. She was going to enjoy her reprieve. Who knew if she would get another one?

# CHAPTER 6

The Markanor strode out the side door of his compound. He swiped his forearm over the scanner in his next-door neighbor's wall. The door opened, and he walked in.

"Sorban!" he yelled. "Sorban!"

"What, Mikael? Why are you coming over here yelling, my boy? You'll make me deaf."

He smiled and went to his godfather, and knelt for a moment reverently before him. Once a challenge of courtship had been issued, he could only discuss it with particular individuals. If he wanted to talk, there were only three choices: his parents, her parents, or a godparent.

"I have a problem, Sorban," he said to the older man. Sorban was still somewhat muscular and straight-backed even though he was seventy-five years old.

He told his godfather everything that had happened.

"I wanted to ask advice on how to deal with this woman. I will not take an unwilling partner to bed."

"Of course not, boy. You're a Markan — the Markanor, for goodness sake. You don't need to chase after women who don't want you."

"That's the problem. I'll have to chase after her. I marked her."

"You what?" Sorban's mouth dropped open.

"I issued the challenge of courtship."

"Does that slave know what you've done?" his godfather said, clearly upset.

"No, she's human. And a naive one at that."

"Then you don't have to abide by it. She doesn't even know."

"Sorban," he said. "I would know."

"But why would you do such a thing?"

"I don't know." He sat down on a chair. "She was so afraid of me. I didn't like that. She's different from the others. And she fascinates me somehow."

"So you will be pursuing a slave girl. Never a good idea, Mikael. And especially not a good idea for someone in your position."

"But I want her to be willing to come to my bed. Issuing the challenge doesn't mean I have to marry her or even ask her."

"That's true. But it does suggest that you might consider it."

"Not really," he said. But he could see that his godparent was not convinced. For that matter, neither was he.

He wasn't sure what he was doing, but he knew that he had never met anyone like Lyzette before. She was beautiful, but she seemed unaware of it, which made her more attractive. Her body was unbelievably sexy, and he wanted her badly. On the other hand, she was innocent and apparently inexperienced.

He suddenly wanted to be her first with a desperate longing. He would show her how pleasant it could be to lie with him. He would be the first to plow her fertile field, and she would like it.

"Mikael!" Sorban snapped his fingers in front of Mikael's face. "You're smitten with this slave girl."

"I am not. I only want her body, and I want her to be willing. I'm sure she felt something when I issued the challenge, so it shouldn't be difficult to convince her to want me. How can I make her less afraid of me?"

"You don't need seduction tips from an old man," he said, giving Mikael a sarcastic look.

"No, I don't. I can handle seduction. I need help getting her to the point where she desires to be seduced."

"That I may be able to assist you with," he said. "First, she needs to trust you. Then she needs to like you. The more she likes you, the more she'll want you to seduce her. Touch her casually. Hold her hand. Put your arm around her. Once she trusts and likes you, that is. If she seems to like it, then you can proceed with a chaste kiss or a hug. You take it from there, son."

"Trust, then like, then touch her casually. Got it." He said it as if he were committing it to memory for a test.

His godfather cackled.

"You are smitten."

"I'm not, Sorban. Stop saying that. I want her so bad I can hardly stand it, ever since I saw her in that slave cage. I have no emotional attachment whatsoever."

"If you just wanted to fuck this girl, you wouldn't have needed to issue the challenge."

"Thanks for the advice, Sorban, but I'm late."

"For your date with the slave girl, I know, I know. Bring her over some time. I want to meet the girl who's got you wrapped around her finger."

"I have to go," he said, absentmindedly.

"Be careful. Slave girls can be wily creatures. You have the responsibility for the planet on your shoulders. You can't be getting caught up with some woman."

"I take my responsibilities seriously. You know that. For the last time, I'm not getting caught up in her. I want her body."

"Keep telling yourself that, my boy," his godfather said, shaking his head. "Keep telling yourself and maybe someday you'll believe it. I know I sure as heck won't."

\* \* \*

Lyzette arrived at the stable in a pink crop top. It showed off her torso. Her jeans rode low on her hips, and a pair of sandals graced her delicate feet. She had pulled her hair back into a ponytail. When she saw the Markanor, she actually smiled at him.

"That's better," he said. For the first time, he smiled back, and she nearly stumbled back from the force of it.

He had a brilliant smile.

"What is better?" she asked.

"You don't look scared anymore. It's a vast improvement."

"Oh," Lyzette said, nodding and feeling uncomfortable.

"Let's get going."

"What are we doing?" she asked.

"Going for a ride," he said, walking over to a sturdy looking carriage. It was practical, not flashy, and didn't have all the fancy add-ons that the other ones in the stable did. It was painted black and looked like the man who had designed it cared about function. It has no bling; others had gold trim and scalloped edging.

"I want to show you a bit of Marka."

She didn't know what she had been expecting from the Markanor, but it hadn't been a tour.

He helped her climb into the conveyance and stepped in behind her. They got settled, side by side, and he spoke a word to the coachman. The man slapped the reins on the horses' backs, and the coach moved smoothly forward, pulling them out of the stable and onto the road.

As the vista spread out before them, Lyzette couldn't help but draw in a deep breath. She had never seen anything as beautiful as her surroundings. Earth was polluted, overpopulated, and entirely consumed by urban sprawl. Out here on an alien planet, the view was spectacular. They were on high ground that allowed them to see the entire valley, revealing green fields and snug-looking houses. She could see people working the land. The suns were simultaneously descending towards the horizon and turning everything golden.

Lyzette was enchanted.

"It's lovely. I've never seen anything like it."

"Never?" The Markanor was surprised.

"There isn't anything like this on Earth anymore," she said, sadly. "Too much overcrowding and pollution."

"Well, this is what Marka looks like everywhere. We are a prosperous planet, and we consider the land our most precious resource. We are good stewards."

Lyzette nodded, turning away and gazing at the landscape. After they had been driven in silence for about twenty minutes, the Markanor tapped the coachman on the shoulder and gave him some instructions.

He continued along for some time and then turned onto a road that was no longer dirt but cobblestone. They were in a city, but it was like no city Lyzette had ever seen before. There was greenery everywhere. Flowers spilled out of window boxes. Trees and gardens were all over the place. The houses were tall and had gardens on their roofs.

"How is it that everything looks rustic, and yet you have advanced computers, communications, and space travel?" Lyzette asked in confusion.

"It's by design," the Markanor explained. "When technology and modernization started developing at a rapid pace, our society made the conscious decision to keep our planet unchanged. And that's why you'll see a farmer on his wagon using a computer to talk to his granddaughter who lives four thousand miles away."

"Wow, that's so clever of you," Lyzette said, wiggling around happily. "It's amazing that you managed to take care of your planet and still have all the conveniences of modern life. It seems too good to be true."

"Too good to be true on your planet maybe, but Marka and many others have made the transition without destroying everything. It can be done."

They continued to ride through the city with the Markanor pointing out points of interest for her. And then, unexpectedly, Lyzette's stomach rumbled. Her cheeks turned pink.

"Excuse me," she said.

"You're hungry. Why didn't you say anything?" he said.

She didn't tell him that she had been so afraid at lunch that she hadn't been able to eat. She guessed it would be inappropriate to say she was pretty sure slaves weren't supposed to demand supper. She tried to convey all this information by shrugging her shoulders expressively.

The Markanor tapped the coachman again, and he stopped outside an ancient-looking bar. It reminded her of the night she had been abducted, but she immediately put the thought out of her head. It wouldn't do to think about that right now. Everything was different.

They sat in a booth, and the Markanor ordered for both of them after asking what sort of meat was her favorite.

"How is it that everything is so much like Earth?" she said.

"The Great Race colonized all of the planets in the galaxy, and so we are all genetically identical. Sometimes the Great Race brought plant and animal species that they liked from one planet to another."

Lyzette nodded, trying to look like she knew all about this.

"If the planets they colonized didn't have much food, the people brought their favorites. Earth was colonized first, and those who arrived here decided to plant and raise similar food."

He looked at her for a moment before going on.

"Of course, that was before Earth had the catastrophic event that sent it back into the dark ages, and before it got left behind by all the other planets."

Lyzette had no idea what he was talking about and was afraid that if she said something, she would look stupid. She got the sense everything about the Great Race was known, and she was uneducated. How had she missed that in school? She had flunked out of most classes, but surely she would have heard of this Great Race before now.

She sighed internally at her stupidity and decided not to ask any more questions about Marka. She didn't want to show off her ignorance, so she would ask him about himself. Her mother had always told her that men liked to talk about themselves.

"What exactly is the position of Markanor?" she said, picking up a chip and gently dipping it in ketchup before she bit off the end.

"It's like a king, I guess, you could call it. But of the whole planet."

No wonder everyone was deferential to him. She was frozen with food in her hand, staring at him.

"Don't start looking at me like that again," he said. "Today, I'm just Mikael. You can call me that, okay? Forget about the Markanor thing, unless I order you to do something."

"All right, I will," Lyzette said. She was slowly melting. His cajoling tone and the sweet look on his face pushed her fear away. "If you'll call me by my name, too. It's Lyzette." She had noticed that he hadn't addressed her directly.

Of course, Lyzette hadn't called him anything either, since she couldn't remember any of the instructions that Raimey had given her on the proper way to refer to the Markanor.

"Okay, Lyzette."

"Okay, Mikael," she said.

He lifted his glass, and she clinked it with her own.

As they finished their meal, Lyzette smiled happily. Now that she was getting to know the Markanor, she liked him. Their forearms passed close together again when they touched glasses, and she felt another shiver go through her. It ended up somewhere surprising. For the first time since the attack in the alleyway, Lyzette felt that things were looking up.

The feeling lasted for about three seconds and stopped when a man came up to Mikael and punched him hard in the face, knocking him off his chair.

# CHAPTER 7

Lyzette screamed and jumped up, pushing her chair away. Mikael was already back on his feet. He and his assailant faced off in a small area between the tables. Mikael attacked quickly, throwing his shoulder into the man's stomach, making his breath audibly leave his body. Mikael flipped him over his shoulder, and the man landed flat on his back.

Lyzette palms sweated as she watched. She placed her hand over her mouth when Mikael spun around to face his opponent. He got up slowly and appeared to be winded. Mikael threw a sharp punch to the face. He must have had a lot of experience fighting.

His opponent reached up weakly to block the punch, but the blow had enough power to knock him to his side. Mikael followed his punch with two uppercuts to the chin that looked like they nearly took his head off.

Mikael grabbed his attacker by the hair and kneed him in the face. The knee was finally enough. His enemy fell to the ground, unconscious and bleeding. Mikael watched him fall and then nodded to himself. When he looked back at Lyzette, she was staring at him. She wasn't sure if she should be more afraid of Mikael or his assailant.

"Come on, Lyzette. We should get out of here. I'll explain what happened."

As they approached the exit, the owner of the restaurant waved Mikael past him. Apparently the Markanor didn't have to pay for his meals, or he didn't have to pay for them when he beat up a potential customer. Lyzette wasn't sure which one it was.

He took her by the elbow and steered her out the door and onto the street. When he didn't see the carriage, he cursed. Mikael changed his mind, guiding her towards a nearby park instead. They sat down on a bench next to a finely crafted stone wall.

"Jol will be back momentarily. He's probably doing an errand," Mikael said.

"Sure," Lyzette nodded. "What happened back there? I feel like someone could randomly attack me at any time."

"You have to understand that you're not on Earth anymore, Lyzette, and this is a different culture. There are different rules."

"Yes, of course," she said, trying to look like she knew what he was saying.

"On Earth, I'm under the impression that you place value on one's intelligence."

"Yes." Lyzette knew being smart was important because she wasn't, and that had been hard for her.

"Well, it's not like that on Marka. We prize strength and valor in battle more than anything here. You've seen our civilization is extremely peaceful, but that's on the surface. Below our polite society is a roiling, seething mass of men, fighting to come out on top."

Lyzette leaned forward and listened to him with rapt attention. She had seized on the words roiling and seething but hadn't heard anything else.

"What are you talking about?" she asked.

"Okay, let me explain. There are clans. Everyone belongs to a clan except the Clanless. Without a clan, you might as well leave the planet. These clans are peaceful during everyday life, most of the time. But there is always jockeying for position at the top. Right now our clan is in the best position. That's why I'm the Markanor. But I could be ousted tomorrow if another clan showed enough strength."

"Really?" Lyzette said feeling worried.

"Well, it's possible," he admitted. "But not probable. Usually, a clan holds the power for years or decades. It's not easy to overthrow the clan that's in power because of all the allies involved."

"Do you have wars?"

"No. It's generally small skirmishes. I gained points for our side today. And the points keep me in power."

"From having fights in restaurants." Lyzette said, trying to understand.

Mikael sighed.

"When you say it like that, it sounds a little crazy," he said. "Yes, fights in restaurants or on the street. They could kidnap you, for example. That would give them points because I failed to protect you."

Lyzette blanched.

"I was kidnapped already and sold into slavery," she said, staring down at her hands. "Did that give you points?"

"No, I didn't get any points from that. I'm sorry. I didn't know." He looked at her with troubled eyes and tried to move quickly to another topic. "Anything that reveals my weakness gives them points. There is one house that's a particular thorn in my side — the Delanor. They've always been trying to weaken us, but they haven't been successful. Every point they gain we get back. The man who just attacked me was a Delanor. Who knows what he might have done to you if he had knocked me out," Mikael said. "All in the name of honor for his house."

"It doesn't sound like your culture is very respectful of women," Lyzette said, quietly.

"On the contrary, we prize our women greatly — even slaves. That's why if we fail to protect them, we lose a lot of points. It's a sin for a man to be unable to protect his woman."

At that moment, Jol drove up, and they got into the carriage. He was full of apologies for not being there waiting when Lyzette and Mikael needed him.

The Markanor excused Jol, and they made their way home without further incident.

---

Lyzette learned that Mikael was going to be away from home for two days. He needed to inspect his property and lands in the Northern Hemisphere. She wouldn't have to worry about him for a whole forty-eight hours. As much as she had liked spending time with him, the burden of knowing that she might have to have sex with him had been draining.

Now she didn't have to worry, and she could enjoy herself for a couple days. It was like a vacation, as long as she forgot she was a slave. She hugged herself and danced around her room when Delia told her the news.

"You're *happy* he's going? You're crazy, girl, if you don't want a piece of that man. I wish he still wanted me," she said.

"You were a consort, too?" Lyzette said as she finished making her bed. She started helping Delia wash the windows in her room, and all the rooms in the hallway.

"I was."

"Did you..." Lyzette didn't know how to phrase what she wanted to ask.

"Like it? You bet, girl. Easy days. No big work parties. Just spread my legs and come three or four times a day. I loved it."

Lyzette looked at her open-mouthed.

"I was going to say hate it. Did you hate it."

"Hate it? That's crazy. Are you religious or something, Lyz? You let him touch you once, and you are never going back to your nun-ish ways. I have a feeling that there is a very passionate woman in you, waiting to come out. Look at how quickly you came in the practice session."

Lyzette blushed as she thought about how the women had coached her and showed her how to understand her body. Still, it was an important lesson if her new life revolved around her private parts. She considered it part of her education. It had been horribly embarrassing, though. The mortifying feeling when she felt the rush of orgasm for the first time, and knowing all the women had witnessed it, made her blush even now.

But she didn't expect to feel that way with the Markanor. He was a stranger. She couldn't let him touch those parts, ever.

She still thought she had a choice.

* * *

Two days passed quickly, and Lyzette got anxious when the gossip passed through the slaves that the master had returned. She was asked to dress for a formal dinner. The master wanted to dine with her.

Lyzette nervously did up the front of her dress. It was crimson and had a tight bodice that stayed up with hooks. The corset pushed her breasts up into some incredible cleavage, of course.

The dress had a full skirt that draped all the way to the floor, covering her chunky heels that were red as well. It reminded her of a dress she had wished for back on Earth when she had been window shopping. Becoming a slave, however, was not part of her dream.

The fancy dress had frilly sleeves that tightened along her forearm. She was glad about the tight fit. Lyzette had been deathly afraid that her dress would have trailing sleeves that might trail through her soup. She didn't want to be humiliated again in front of her master. Raimey came and curled her hair, pinning it up in a way that made Lyzette look lovely.

When she felt ready, she made her way downstairs to the formal dining room. There wasn't a long table like she had expected. It was big, but there were only two places set at one end. Mikael wasn't there when she walked in, so she adjusted her dress and waited, trying not to fidget.

"Lyzette." She heard his voice behind her and the feelings his voice evoked in her were surprising. She turned, smiled, and managed a graceful curtsy. She had practiced all day. Maureen had taught her.

"Hello," she said, politely.

"How have you been?" he said, and she took his arm the way Raimey had tutored her. He led her to the table, and a servant pulled out her chair for her.

"Fine," she said, feeling tongue-tied.

The meal passed with stilted conversation and long silences. Lyzette wondered where the unusual man who had taken her on the tour of his home had gone. When the servants took the last course away, he stood up and extended his hand. She took it, reminding herself that she was his slave, and she had to do what he wanted her to.

He led her to another room that was considerably smaller and dimmer.

"What are we doing?" she said.

"You will have to attend several formal occasions with me throughout the year, so I thought we could practice dancing."

"I'm not terribly good at dancing," she said. She had no idea what to do.

"You'll never get better unless you try." Mikael wore dark pants and a coat that buttoned with gold buttons. He looked handsome. He went to a shelf and turned on music.

A song played throughout the room, and he led her through the steps of a traditional Markan folk dance. She felt like she had two left feet, but soon he had her laughing and relaxed. She squealed and clapped her hands when she finally learned it.

"You're quite graceful, Lyzette," he said.

"I'm not," she said, making a face. "My mother always told me I was as graceful as a cat taking a shit."

"Your mother doesn't sound very kind," Mikael said.

"She's not," Lyzette said matter-of-factly.

"Okay, one last dance," Mikael said, changing the music.

A slow song came on.

"Come here," he said, placing her hands on his shoulders and putting his hands on her hips.

"I don't think we need to practice this kind of dance," she said. Her breathing came faster when he was close, and she couldn't stop thinking about the way he was looking at her.

"On the contrary," he said, tugging her a tiny bit closer to him so that her nipples brushed his chest. She tried not to gasp or show any reaction as she felt them harden.

What was going on with her body? "It's imperative to get this dance right."

"Because it's vertical foreplay?" Lyzette said.

He looked startled and laughed, pulling her close and hugging her. Lyzette lost her breath. After the hug, he kept his body pressed up along the length of hers.

The music was slow and beautiful. She got lost in the sound and the feeling of him. She loved the way he gazed soulfully into her eyes.

"Lyzette," he breathed.

She stared at him.

"I'm going to kiss you now."

She nodded mutely, completely in his thrall. There was no way for her to stop him. After all, she didn't want him to stop.

He slowly bent his head and pressed his lips to hers. It was a chaste kiss. She felt a thrill go through her whole body, and she drew in a quick breath, opening her mouth. When she did this, she felt his tongue dart out and touch hers.

The effect of his tongue was electric and this time the thrill went directly to her core. She made a tiny sound, and unable to hold back she twisted her tongue with his.

Her breathing was warm and erratic as her heartbeat sped up.

Wait.

She wasn't supposed to be letting him touch her.

She was supposed to be keeping him far away for as long possible, so he would leave her alone. He would think that she wanted him to take her jewel if she kept kissing him like this.

Lyzette pulled away unexpectedly, taking two or three steps away.

"Mikael," she said, her breathing unsteady. "I have to go."

She fled the room, not caring what he thought, but she hoped he wouldn't come after her for more.

# CHAPTER 8

The next morning was uneventful. Lyzette's plan was to hide out in the orchard and avoid Mikael. She knew she ought to be helping with the chores, but she promised herself that she would work harder for the next few days in exchange for one day of shirking.

She wandered through acres of fruit trees and snacked on different varieties of Markan fruit. She hoped it was all edible. Otherwise, they would find her dead. By afternoon, she was sleepy and lay down in a warm spot, wrapped up in a shawl. Soon she was fast asleep.

When she woke, she felt strange and disoriented. She didn't know where she was or what had woken her.

"Mother?" she said, sitting up and looking around.

"I must have stepped on a twig and disturbed you," Mikael said. "I'm sorry. You looked beautiful sleeping there."

Beautiful? He thought she was beautiful? Attractive maybe, on a good day, with make-up on. She certainly didn't feel beautiful after getting up from a nap with grass in her hair and nothing but the sunshine on her face.

"Thank you," she whispered. She shifted herself so she could lean against a tree.

"May I?" he said, indicating the ground next to her.

Did he want to sit beside her? That was probably a bad idea. But he was her master. Who was she to tell him where to sit?

She nodded.

"Are you hiding from me?" he asked. He sat beside her so that their legs touched all along the length. Lyzette was distracted and couldn't answer right away.

"No, of course not," she said. Immediately she knew she had not fooled him. "Maybe."

"You're afraid of me." He played with the grass and didn't look at her, but she sensed he was worried about her answer.

"I'm not afraid of you."

"What are you afraid of, then?" He tilted his head to meet her eye.

She didn't say anything.

He took her hand and interlaced their fingers. She took a deep breath and tried to stay calm.

"Does this bother you?" he said, studying her reaction.

She shook her head.

"You like it?"

"A little." She was unable to lie when he looked directly at her.

"Good." They sat there for the better part of an hour until it was time to go for dinner. He held her hand as they walked back to the house and told her stories of his adventures as a boy, completely charming her.

She had to remind herself he was her master, not her boyfriend.

---

That night someone knocked on Lyzette's door. She wore her pajamas and sat on the balcony sketching Mikael from memory. She shoved the drawing pad under the mattress by habit and went to the entryway.

It was Mikael, wearing plaid pajama pants and a T-shirt. He held up a pack of cards.

"Want to play?" he asked.

Lyzette smiled a little. She wasn't very good at cards, but if he wanted to play, she couldn't say no. Her job was pleasing the Markanor — Mikael, she reminded herself.

"Sure." She opened the door and allowed him to come in. As his body went past hers, she felt the heat coming off of him and caught the scent of his soap. It gave her a strange feeling that she didn't recognize. She remained at the door, not closing it.

"Everything okay, Lyzette?" he said, looking as if he found something amusing.

"Yes. Everything's fine."

He sat down at the breakfast table. It was located in a corner of her bedroom, next to the desk and armchair. He dealt out the cards, and Lyzette sat across from him, watching his skillful hands flying as the cards landed neatly in piles in front of himself and her. Then he explained a Markan card game to her, which seemed to involve a lot of touching.

"I know it looks weird because you're human, but ask anyone impartial. Jol or the cook. They will tell you it's true. We're a physical people, Lyzette. You'll have to get used to it." His blue eyes were dancing.

She tried to keep the rules straight, but when she lost her first tile and had to hold her right hand on his left shoulder, she started to get distracted. And when he lost two tiles and had to put his bare foot on hers and put his left hand on her right arm, she wasn't sure if they were still playing a game. Was he making these rules up?

"Part of the fun is getting criss-crossed while you still try to handle your cards," he said, clearly enjoying himself. It reminded her of a sick cross between Twister and poker.

"There's a game that the young men and women play that involves removing clothing instead of getting twisted up. Want to play that version?" he said. He laughed and was obviously joking. Lyzette missed the joke. She was trying to figure out if she was going to lose the next tile or not, and she wasn't looking at him.

"Sure." All she remembered was that she was supposed to be agreeable. She wasn't paying attention to what she agreed to.

"Really?" he said, not quite believing her.

Uh oh. What had she just agreed to? Lyzette looked up from her cards.

"Yes, of course. Whatever you want to play," she said, hoping it wasn't too awful.

"Okay then," he said, and they untwisted their limbs.

Lyzette bit her lip and laid down three cards. Mikael winced.

"Are you sure you want to do that?" he said.

"Not anymore," Lyzette responded, grimacing.

Mikael laughed.

"But I'll learn faster if you don't coddle me," she said. "That's what Mother always said. She said if she made me face my lumps then I'd figure things out faster. But I never did. I guess I've lost this tile?"

"You did."

"And what do I have to do?"

"Take off any piece of your clothing," he said, watching her face to see her reaction. She felt uncomfortable, but she had played games like this before at parties.

"Like strip poker. The guys used to like playing that with me," Lyzette said.

"I'll bet," Mikael said, under his breath.

She was about to take her pants off but hesitated. She looked at him, trying to see his reaction.

"You don't have to play this version if you don't want to, Lyzette," he said.

She shook her head.

"It's okay."

She removed her pants, leaving her tiny baby blue cotton panties. These were her most comfortable sleeping clothes.

She saw him draw in a deep breath. Yes, the men always liked playing games like this with her. She had a feeling that if she lost this time, she'd lose more than her clothing, and she wasn't sure she would mind.

Still, she could focus and play to win. Mikael had the advantage being familiar with the game, but maybe

Lyzette could be clever if she concentrated. She paid attention, and on the next round won a tile from him.

He pulled off his shirt.

She should have paid more attention to the rules of the game. Lyzette looked at his broad chest, his defined six pack, and chiseled biceps. She wanted to run her hands over him. She didn't know what was coming over her.

He was looking at her at the same time. They watched each other secretly as he dealt. Each movement flexed muscles all over his torso. Lyzette managed to pull her eyes away to focus on the cards. She was determined to win this tile, too. The cards were against her, and she couldn't have won no matter what she did.

"I lost," she said.

"Yep. It's a shame." A corner of his mouth lifted up.

So, what should it be? The shirt or the panties? She tried to decide. Either way would bare private parts to Mikael that she hadn't planned on showing him ever. Full frontal nudity would be a distraction for him. She might win the next tile, and he would have to take off his pants.

She wondered if he was wearing anything underneath.

Making the decision, she crossed her arms over her chest and grabbed the hem of her shirt. Then with a quick, graceful movement she pulled the whole thing off and tossed it on the floor. Her breasts, she knew, were one of her best features, and her mother always taught her to flaunt them. Of course, they were usually covered, but the principle still held. She sat up straight, knowing they were full and round.

He would undoubtedly lose his tile this time.

Mikael swallowed hard, and Lyzette felt her nipples harden as he looked at her. The fresh breeze on her exposed breasts tickled, and she felt a tingle that went all the way down between her legs. Raimey had said that he wouldn't even touch her unless she begged him.

Strangely, she was beginning to feel that she might want to beg.

But not yet.

Lyzette dealt the cards this time, knowing that her soft mounds were jiggling with every throw of the card. She watched as Mikael played, knowing that she had this tile. She smiled triumphantly and played her last card.

"I win," she said.

"No kidding," Mikael said sarcastically, looking directly at her breasts on display before him. Then he pulled off his pants.

She saw with disappointment that he was wearing boxers. He must have seen it on her face.

"Are you sorry that I have underwear on, Lyzette?" He had a mildly predatory look on his face. She felt a funny feeling down between her legs again, but she ignored it.

"Yes. I mean, no. Maybe a bit. But it's okay. I'm going to win the next one, and then you won't be wearing anything."

"Or I will, and you won't be wearing anything."

"No, I've got this figured out. I'm going to win," Lyzette said.

Mikael dealt, and they both paid close attention to the cards. After a few minutes, it became obvious who would win the tile. Lyzette tried every strategy he had taught her, but it was all in vain.

"I win," he said, his blue eyes darkening.

"You did," she said. "And fair's fair."

She stood up then and hooked her thumbs in her panties. Mikael watched spellbound as she shimmied them down over her hips and stepped out of them. She lifted her chin and stood naked in front of him, wondering what would happen next and if she wanted it or not.

His hot gaze travelled down to her breasts. They looked swollen and aroused. Then his eyes dipped lower to where her sex lay nestled between her creamy thighs.

"You're beautiful, Lyzette," he said, his voice sounding a little rougher than usual. Her own eyes dropped momentarily to his boxers, and she saw that something was bulging down there.

"What happens now?" she said, meeting his gaze anxiously.

"Whatever you want."

"So, if I told you to leave, you would," she said, clearly not believing it.

"Yes," he said, his eyes burning into hers. "Do you want me to go, Lyzette?"

She thought for a long time and finally, she shivered and sat down again.

"No. I want to play another round. And you better not lose on purpose, Mikael," she said, pointing at him.

He grinned.

"I don't like to lose, Lyzette. You should know that by now," he said.

She thought of the courtship challenge. Well, he should know that she didn't like to lose either.

His underwear was coming off. She wanted to see what was in his pants.

# CHAPTER 9

Lyzette didn't like to lose. But she usually did.

"Now what?" Lyzette asked. "I have nothing left to take off."

"How about a kiss instead?" Mikael suggested. His breathing quickened at the thought.

"A kiss?" she said.

"You kiss me. You're in control of everything."

"I can kiss you however I want?"

"Yes, but it has to be lips on lips."

Lyzette pressed her lips together, brows furrowed.

"Okay," she decided.

She stood up, and she noticed that his bulge jumped as her entire body was put on display again. She bit her lip and walked around the table until she was almost touching him.

"You'll have to come a little closer, Lyzette, if you're going to kiss me," he said.

"Would you mind standing up?" Lyzette asked. It would be better if she didn't have to bend over and stick her boobs in his face.

He stood up, and she suddenly faced a wall of muscle. She put her hands on his shoulders and stretched up on her tiptoes to place her lips on his.

She miscalculated. It was impossible for her to kiss him without her breasts brushing his chest. And as she pressed her lips to his, her nipples came into contact with his hot skin.

She gasped, and all of a sudden what was intended to be a quick peck became something more. He didn't insist on more, but she felt herself responding against her will. Unintentionally, Lyzette's tongue darted out and touched his. She moaned and wrapped her arms around his neck, pressed her breasts against him, and tangled her tongue in his mouth.

Her thinking mind shut down. She forgot all about the card game, and completely focused on this man and his body on hers.

A door slammed down the hall, and the noise jolted them. She pulled back suddenly and stared at Mikael, who was blinking like he was trying to remember who he was, too. Her breasts tingled. In her sex was not a tingle, but an ache.

She wanted more of something, but she didn't know what. She knew it had to do with him taking her jewel.

They gazed at each other.

"Let's play," Mikael said hoarsely. Lyzette sat down on her chair with a thump — as if her legs could no longer hold her.

She was sure that he would win again. She hoped he would if it meant he would make her kiss him again. They both looked up in surprise when she took the tile.

"You win," Mikael said. "In more ways than one."

Oh? Was he so enjoyable to see? Really?

He stood up, slowly and once he was upright, she couldn't keep her eyes off his underwear.

Slowly he put his fingers in and pulled the front of his boxers out and over what turned out to be an enormous thing. She didn't even know what to call it. It looked colossal. At the end, it was shiny and round. She couldn't believe how big it was.

She knew that men liked their things to be big and that some women said it was important for men to be big. But the only thing on her mind was, how in God's name would he ever fit that thing inside of her. And how would she survive it?

\* \* \*

She licked her lips nervously.

"Lyzette." She knew he had said her name, but she couldn't stop looking at it. "Lyzette."

She glanced up at him then.

"Yes?"

"The game usually goes on to one more tile. This is the last round. If you lose, I get to touch you. And if I lose, you get to touch me."

She nodded, then frowned.

"It seems like you win no matter what."

"Are you saying that you don't want to touch me? I could leave now."

"No," she said quickly, putting a hand out towards him as if she could keep him from moving. "No. You don't have to go. I want to finish the game."

He grinned, and he looked satisfied. They played quickly, both of them intent on the cards. Finally, Lyzette laid her last two cards down.

Shit. She lost.

Mikael put away the game.

"Come here," he said, and took her hand, leading her to the bed. "Lie down."

"What are you going to do?" Lyzette asked nervously.

"Do you trust me, Lyzette?" he said, looking her straight in the eye.

"Yes," she said. She was surprised to realize that it was true.

"Then lie down on the bed," he said. "Fair's fair. I get to touch you."

She lay down, and he went and turned out the lights. He went next to her without touching her.

Lyzette lay on her back, her arms crossed over her chest and her legs tight together. Mikael lay on his side. He scooted over so that his body was touching hers along the entire length.

He let her become comfortable until he felt her muscles relax.

"May I touch you, Lyzette?" he said.

She didn't know what that meant. But it sounded like a good idea, in spite of how anxious she was feeling. She nodded.

He ran his hand down her cheek, tracing her jawline. Then one finger traced a line between her breasts where they quivered on her chest, longing for him to touch them.

But he didn't.

He spread his large hand out on her belly and rubbed in a couple lazy circles before he continued skimming down her leg to her foot and back up.

When he returned, he slid his hand up along the inside of her thigh. When she thought he would touch her mound, he lifted his hand over and landed again on her flat stomach, going up the far side of her torso, barely brushing her skin with his palm.

She drew in a deep breath and by the light of the moons coming in the windows she saw her breasts, silver in the moonlight, rise and fall. Mikael leaned over and kissed her then, a gentle, teasing, exploratory kiss that seemed to go on forever and made the aching between her legs worse.

They kissed for a long time until Lyzette felt frustrated that he wouldn't touch her where she needed him to. Then she remembered what Raimey had said about her begging him.

And without thinking, she took his hand off of her hip and placed it directly on her breast, where he cupped it without thinking.

"You're sure, Lyzette," he said, lifting his head to look her in the eyes.

"I'm sure," she said. "I trust you, Mikael. It aches down there."

"Oh, Lyzzie. I'll take care of that, if you want me to," he said.

"Just do it, Mikael. Just do it. Now."

But he didn't.

He continued his slow exploration of her body. But finally, his mouth closed over her nipple and sucked. And Lyzette thought she would come just from that. It felt so damn good. She moaned and her hips bucked. He moved to her other breast, and he pleasured her so thoroughly that she thought she would die until his hand slid lightly down her body and cupped her sex.

She gasped and clenched her legs tighter.

"Spread for me, Lyzzie," he said. And it sounded so dirty that it only made Lyzette want him more. She spread her legs a little bit, and his hand slipped in, opening her petals. But her thighs must still have been too tight together for his liking because he wedged his knee in between and pushed them wide apart.

Her breathing was erratic and her thoughts jumbled. Was she going to let him take her jewel? Was it even her decision to make? She had to submit to him, didn't she? The slaves needed her to. And besides, she was a slave herself, not a free woman, and she had no choice. If he wanted to take her, he could.

At that instant, his finger found a hard little nub at the top of her folds.

"Ohhhh," she said, breathily as he began circling it.

That was the spot that the women had called the clitoris or clit. And she remembered how touching it had brought her first orgasm.

She didn't have to wait long. In her state of arousal, after a few minutes of stimulation, she was seized by a rush of sensation so intense, she cried out, her body spasming several times.

"Did you just come?" Mikael said in amazement.

After she had got her breath back, Lyzette nodded.

"Yes."

"Holy shit," he said.

"The women said I was orgasmic."

"You certainly are," he said. "But now I want to see a G-spot orgasm."

She felt her sex clench in anticipation.

"What's that?" she said.

"You'll see," he said, crawling down her body, kissing her everywhere as he went.

Why was he going down there?

Then she remembered Raimey's advice not to put too much scent down there because he didn't like to taste it. But she hadn't thought she was serious.

At the first touch of his tongue on her clit, her hips drove up into his face. His large hands pressed her down to the bed, restraining her as he went to work. His tongue swirled gently around until she felt the heat starting to build again. He dropped back down and licked up the length of her several times. He frequently returned to her hard nub to tease her over and over.

Without any warning, she felt his finger sliding into her opening.

"Oh, what are you doing?" she said.

He didn't answer but slid his finger in farther. She sucked in a breath and stayed still as he continued probing her. His tongue never stopped moving on her. It was uncomfortable having his finger inside her, but she didn't tell him to stop. He pushed further in until he came to a barrier — her jewel.

She wriggled a little as she felt her orgasm building. Then inexplicably Mikael slowed his tongue down and sucked gently, while his finger rubbed up on the top inside wall of her hole. At first she didn't feel anything and was disappointed that he wasn't going to make her come again.

But then she felt something, and the something felt so good that she pressed her hips towards him and urged him to continue. He rubbed faster, and his tongue began its relentless circling again. She shuddered in completion, groaning, her hips grinding up on his face, riding on a wave of frenzy that seemed to go on and on.

After she got quiet, he crawled back up and lay against her again.

"That was wonderful," she said. "Can we do it again?"

Mikael chuckled.

"We haven't done it yet, Lyzzie."

"We haven't?" she said. "There's more than that?"

"We're just getting started," he said, kissing her cheek.

She blew out a big breath. He turned towards her, wrapping his arms around her and sliding one leg between hers, twisting his body into hers.

Bring it on, she thought.

# CHAPTER 10

He took such a long time leading up to it that Lyzette thought she would go mad with longing.

"Please, Mikael." She realized she was begging. "Please do it. I need you inside me."

"Lyzzie, I need to be inside you, too, but first I want to make sure you're going to enjoy it," he said. He got up, leaving her feeling bereft. He returned in a moment carrying a tube.

"What's that?" she asked.

"It is something that will numb you so it won't hurt when I break your maidenhead," he said. "It's a local anesthetic, designed for this purpose."

She had heard sex was going to hurt, and she was glad it would be painless. She heard him take the cap off. She watched as he squeezed a large amount onto his fingers. He pushed two fingers up inside her and rubbed the stuff on the barrier, her jewel.

"It only acts on the tissue of hymen, so it won't actually affect your pleasure," he said. "It won't numb anything else."

She didn't care how it worked.

"Please, Mik? Now?" she said, rubbing her hips against his and feeling his large cock sliding along her slit. Then she thought of something. "What about protection?"

"Protection?"

"So I don't get pregnant," she explained.

"Why would you not want to get pregnant?"

"Never mind," she said, and she spread her legs wide, needing him to fill her.

He slid two fingers back inside of her and pumped them in and out. Yes, that was what she needed. But it wasn't enough. He pushed a third in, and it felt quite uncomfortable, but soon she was thrusting her pelvis against his hand, needing more.

"Mikael," she said, desperately. She reached out and grabbed his hardness. He hissed when she did. She immediately let it go. "Did I hurt you?"

He laughed.

"No, baby. You never touched me before, and it feels incredible."

"Can I touch you again?" she said, tentatively.

"Not now, sweetie. If you do, I might not make it inside of you. Do you want me inside you?"

"Yes, yes, please," she said, almost crying with need.

He came on top of her and lined himself up with her entrance. She closed her eyes, focusing on the feelings. His round tip pressed in, and she gasped at how thick he felt.

"Fuck, you're tight, Lyzzie."

"Is that bad?" she gasped, barely having the breath to talk.

"No. That's good. How does it feel?"

"Just put it in, please, Mik," she said.

He pushed in another inch, and she thought she couldn't take any more but then her body accommodated him, and he pressed in until he came up against her barrier. He kissed her until she was panting and then he gave one hard thrust, piercing her. He filled her completely and was embedded deep inside her body. She thought that her mind blew at that point, but then he began to move.

"Fuck," she said, as he pulled out and drove into her again. "Yes, yes." She couldn't believe she was begging for it. She had never thought that she would enjoy it. She had been wrong.

He found a rhythm and soon she was moving against him, hot and wet. Her voice hardly seemed like her own as she sighed and made little mewling sounds.

Soon she recognized the feeling of an orgasm starting to build again. He increased the tempo and she tilted her hips to get more comfortable. The shift made it so that he was hitting her clit with every driving thrust. He bent down and took one tight nipple in his mouth, sucking and nipping.

Yes, that was it.

Slowly, slowly, she felt it building relentlessly as he pounded her, fast and frantic. She squirmed against him. Almost. Almost.

With one last thrust, she felt her sex convulse as her climax shattered her.

"Lyz, I can't wait any longer." She felt him explode, and his seed filled her.

But her body was not nearly done. There was a frenzy of pulsing, shuddering spasms that rocked her over and over. He had pinned her to his bed as his orgasm finished but she writhed under him for several minutes until with a sigh, she lay entirely still.

She felt relaxed. She wondered if she had ever felt this good before.

"Was that it?" she whispered.

"That, my dear Lyzzie, was most definitely it," he said.

\* \* \*

When Lyzette awoke, she stretched luxuriously and opened her eyes to see Mikael watching her. She immediately felt embarrassed and pulled the sheet up over her breasts.

He didn't say anything, but pulled her closer to him and kissed her again. She melted under his attentions. When he stopped, she smiled shyly up at him.

"You have it, I guess," she said.

"What are you talking about?"

"My jewel," she whispered. "My mother told me to give it to someone special."

She looked up and met his eyes.

"I guess I gave it to you."

He looked at her thoughtfully.

"Are you sorry, Lyz?" he said. "Is there someone back home you would rather have given it to?"

She shook her head.

"No one. I'm glad it was you," she said.

"You enjoyed it?" he said, a smile playing around his lips.

"I did," she whispered into his chest.

"Do you think you might want to do it again?"

"I think I will want to do it again. Over and over," she said.

He laughed and looked at her like she was the most amazing creature he had ever seen. No one had ever looked at her like that. Her mother had only looked at her in disgust or disappointment. Men had only looked at her with lust.

But Mikael made her feel like she was something special, and she liked it.

"Are you sticky, Lyzzie? Do you want to have a shower?"

"Yes," she said and got up to go to the bathroom. She was surprised when he followed her.

"I'm sticky too," he said.

His thing looked different. "Is something wrong with it?"

"No, Lyzette. That's what happens. It doesn't stay up all the time."

"Oh."

"Just when I'm interested in sex."

Lyzette went into the large shower stall and turned the water on hot. He followed and stood behind her so that her back was facing him. Soon the double heads were spraying them simultaneously. She picked up the bar of soap, but Mikael took it from her. She turned her head, raising her eyebrows.

"What are you doing?" she said.

"Washing you," he responded, sliding the bar of soap down her back and over her butt. "I'd think that was obvious."

Her breath came faster, and she felt a tingle in her clit.

"But I'm the slave. Shouldn't I be washing you?" she said. She panted as the bar of soap came back up and around to rub on her nipples. They went from soft, loose peaks to tight round rosebuds in a matter of seconds.

"You can do me later. And if you keep making love to me the way you did, I'll be your slave forever," he whispered into her ear, sliding the slippery soap into her folds and making her gasp.

Lyzette felt something hard pressing into her butt. She twisted around to see what it was and was pleased to discover that Mikael's cock was standing erect. She had been worried that it wouldn't be able to do that again.

Good. She wanted him to take her again. It had felt very, very pleasurable.

The washing was long and thorough. By the time they ended up clean, dry, and back in her bed, they were both hot and quickly losing control. They knelt on the bed, kissing and touching each other.

Mikael roughly pushed her head down on the bed and came around behind her. He lifted her hips up and her round, soft ass was completely bared to him. She felt totally exposed in a way that she hadn't the first time. His knob brushed her sex and she bucked back against him.

With a groan, he took her, filling her with one quick thrust. She wasn't sure she liked it until he started pounding into her, his pelvis slamming against her ass.

His hand came around and touched her button and soon she was coming again as he slid into her over and over. She pressed herself back against him as he continued to plunge into her. She convulsed around him, and he came wildly and explosively — pushing hard against her butt as he gasped, finding his release.

They were so exhausted after their passion that they lay down and curled up together, falling deeply asleep.

---

When Lyzette woke up, Mikael was dressing in the gray light of dawn. She watched him and felt sleepy.

"I have to go, Lyz. But I'll be back later. I have a match, and you can come watch."

She nodded.

He came over and kissed her. Then he walked over to the door, stopped, came back, and kissed her again. It was passionate. She thought that he would want to do it again, but he pulled himself away with a groan.

"I have to go, Lyzette. But I would rather stay here and make love to you again."

She sighed and smiled, her eyes closing again already as he slipped out the door.

When she opened them again, both suns were well past the windows and Raimey was bringing in her breakfast.

"Hello, sleepyhead. I don't know why you slept so late, but I saved you some breakfast when I was cleaning up, thinking you might be hungry when you woke." She stopped suddenly and sniffed the air.

Lyzette watched her.

"It smells like sex in here," she said, going to open the windows.

Lyzette had a self-conscious smile on her face.

"You did it?"

She smiled excitedly at Raimey and nodded.

"Oh, thank goodness. I thought you fucked it up and were going to get shipped back. That's wonderful, Lyz."

Lyzzie felt hurt at the mention of how she had almost messed everything up. She couldn't have wished for anything different because last night was perfect.

"Did you come?"

"Yes," Lyzzie said, sitting up and pulling the sheet up to hide her nakedness. "Three times."

"Three? Oh, you are such a lucky bitch, Lyz," Raimey said.

Lyzette wanted to say something, but she didn't know what to say.

Raimey looked away for a moment and then when she looked back she had a smile fixed firmly in place. She didn't seem quite as cheerful as before. It suddenly occurred to Lyzette that Raimey had been the last consort.

"That's great, Lyzette. Well, if he had you up half the night fucking, you'll be hungry. Eat until you're full and then come down. We have some work to do. Even though you're the consort, you still have to do your fair share when he doesn't want to sleep with you."

"Of course," Lyzette said, moving over to the side of the bed.

Raimey left. Lyzette went and took another shower, remembering the previous night and how wonderful it had been.

She felt uneasy about Raimey. She seemed friendly in general but occasionally she was decidedly unfriendly. Was she jealous because Lyzette had ousted her from her position as Mikael's consort?

Her mother had told her most single women would be jealous when Lyzette landed a man because that meant they couldn't. That might be true in this case because after all, she had the man that all the former consorts still wanted. She frowned but pushed the thought out of her head.

Her job was to please the Markanor. She had done her job last night.

Raimey ought to be pleased with her, Lyzette thought. If he enjoyed her in bed, then she was that much closer to marriage. And if she married him, then she could free the slaves. But Mikael would never marry her, the notion was complete and utter nonsense.

With a smile, Lyzette gave thanks that she was Mikael's consort. She wondered what tonight might bring.

# CHAPTER 11

They rode down the same road in the same carriage as yesterday, but today everything was different.

Lyzette stared down at her legs. Her creamy thighs emerged from a short lavender colored gown — mini-skirts were all the fashion on Marka right now. She wore a matching lavender blouse. It buttoned up and tied under her breasts, leaving her midsection showing. Her slightly sore breasts, in the push-up bra, showed the two pure white mounds because the top button on the blouse wasn't buttoned up.

"Lyzette, can we stop for a minute?" Mikael said, his icy blue eyes on fire again.

"Why?" she said.

"I need you," he whispered in her ear, and she smiled.

He asked the coachman to stop and then pulled her by the hand. They followed a beaten dirt path, down a steep hill, until they came out to a beautiful waterfall.

"Wow!"

"Come here," he said, ignoring the view and tugging on her hand. He led her to the waterfall through a hidden entrance.

"Mikael," she said in amazement. But he kissed her and pushed her hard up against the rock. And she responded again like the night before. His hands slid up under her blouse.

"This shirt makes me crazy. I've wanted to put my hands in here since I saw you."

Her breath hitched as he palmed her breasts through her bra, making the nipples stand up hard and round. He pulled his hands out for a moment and untied and unbuttoned the blouse. He unhooked the bra as well, so her ripe breasts tumbled out into his hot hands.

"And this skirt," he whispered, kissing her neck and dropping his hands to her hips. "Barely covering your gorgeous ass."

Cupping her butt, he pulled her against him so she could feel his erection.

"Mikael," she gasped.

He hiked the skirt up and grinned when he saw she was wearing a tiny thong, at Raimey's insistence. She said there would be panty lines, but now Lyzette realized she might have imagined this happening.

"Perfect," he muttered. "Don't even have to take them off."

His hand slid into her panties and Lyzette's eyes rolled up into her head as he touched her little button. In two minutes, she was panting and ready. He pulled down his pants, letting them fall at his feet.

Showing his impressive strength, Mikael lifted her up by the ass. He didn't bother removing her thong. He slipped the thin piece of material aside and lined himself up, impaling her on his shaft.

Lyzette cried out at the feeling of having him filling her completely. But before she could react, he started pumping into her — pushing her against the rock with each thrust.

"Mikael," she gasped out as she felt the pleasure starting to build. "What if someone sees us?"

"You better come quickly, then," he said, thrusting harder and faster.

She felt completely exposed with her breasts falling out of her shirt and her skirt up around her waist. Mikael's body covered her privates, but there would be no question of what they were doing. If someone came sightseeing at the waterfall, they would get an eyeful.

At the thought, Lyzette's arousal ratcheted up several notches. When Mikael bent and sucked her breast into his mouth, she felt herself fly over the edge, biting her lip so she wouldn't make any noise.

Mikael drove into her several more times and then pushed her to the rock, hard, as she felt him filling her with his seed. Lyzette wondered if she could get pregnant from an alien. There were some children around the mansion, and she wondered how many of them were Mikael's.

As soon as he came, he pulled out of her and did up his pants. In a blissful haze, Lyzette tried repeatedly to latch her bra without success. Mikael took pity on her and helped with the bra as well as her blouse. Then he adjusted her thong and pulled down her skirt.

"Can you walk?" he asked.

Lyzette nodded blankly and though her legs were wobbly, she managed to make it back to the carriage. Soon they were seated, and she recovered enough to be able to look at her surroundings and talk.

They arrived at the city again by early afternoon. Michael's match started at three o'clock. He tried to explain what was going to happen, but Lyzette didn't understand. It involved a lot of pushing and shoving.

Lyzette was glad to be riding in the carriage next to Mikael. Their knees kept bumping, and she couldn't help but smile happily every time. She knew she was setting herself up to get hurt if he dumped her. He was handsome, strong, and big. All of him.

Every few minutes, she flashed back to a moment from behind the waterfall or the night before, which made her want Mikael again. She wondered if she was a slut for wanting him to make love to her again so soon. Her mother told her only sluts liked lots of sex and gave away their jewel to the first guy that tried to spread their legs.

Lyzette sighed. She didn't care. Her mother wasn't here, and Mikael was. He pointed out another Markan sight, and she looked avidly. She was fascinated with this world, now that it seemed to be treating her so kindly.

Her life had never been as good as it was now. Mikael was kind to her and rocked her world when he made love to her. She had a fantastic room in a mansion. She didn't have to work or have old guys with no hair and pot bellies shoving bills down her cleavage, asking for another pitcher of beer. She didn't have her mother criticizing her or making her feel like she had done something wrong, no matter how hard Lyzette tried to please her.

It was a beautiful day, and both suns were shining.

Then a thought occurred to her, and Lyzette's carefully constructed dream world came crashing down as she remembered the one thing that she could not afford to forget.

She was a slave.

And she had to have sex with Mikael. It didn't matter if she liked it or not. She didn't have a choice. She realized he had taken her out yesterday so she would feel comfortable with him. That way, she wouldn't be afraid of having sex with him anymore. He probably figured he was persuasive enough so once she liked him and trusted him, he could easily convince her to give up her jewel. She had done so easily and without a thought.

Well, he was pretty amazing, and she was a fool, but she didn't have a choice. It may have seemed as though she did, but she didn't have any choice at all. She was his fucking slave.

Lyzette felt her carefully constructed bubble pop around her. He hadn't made love to her because he cared about her. He fucked her because she was his property, and he had needs. She suddenly felt dirty and used. All the wonder and amazement of what their bodies did together seemed soiled, and Lyzette was on the verge of tears. Then the tears came out. To conceal them, she turned and looked out of the carriage as if she were enjoying the view.

Mikael didn't notice her change of mood until he had talked to himself about Marka for over twenty minutes. He got a nod from Lyzette every once in a while.

"Lyzette?" he asked, taking her chin and turning her head towards him. She looked at him, not because she wanted to, but because she was his slave, and he wanted her to do something. Tears ran down her cheeks.

He frowned in consternation.

"What's wrong?" he said.

She shook her head. She shifted on the seat and tried to get comfortable. As much as she had enjoyed having sex both times, she was surprised at how sore she was down there. It was a good thing he made sure that it hadn't hurt when he broke her hymen. Otherwise, she would never have enjoyed any of it. But the anesthetic had long worn off, and she felt every bump in the road. Especially now that the euphoria from the waterfall had worn off.

"Lyzette, tell me," he said.

She did because he ordered her to, and she was his slave and had to do everything he said. But she didn't tell him the whole truth.

"I'm sore, from, you know," she whispered. "And I'm trying to keep in mind that I am a slave. I was starting to get some crazy ideas in my head, and I want to keep my feet on the ground. My mother always said that a girl with her head in the clouds gets it knocked off by the first passing jet or shit on by the geese."

Mikael looked shocked. Then he laughed, but his smile faded quickly.

"This is my life. I accept it. There's nothing a person can do to change their lot in life. My mother told me over and over, Lyzette, make the best of it because this is as good as it gets, and you can't change it."

"Lyzette."

"I mean," she went on as if he hadn't even said anything. "I guess I had it a bit better back home because I wasn't a slave and could do what I wanted. But I was just as trapped because I had to work a job I hated. I was asked to sleep with an asshole. My mother was never really happy with me, no matter what I did. And the city was so dirty and ugly. At least here, it's pretty, I have a beautiful room and pretty clothes."

"Lyzette, please, let me say something." he said, trying to stem the flow of words, but she wasn't done.

"You're very nice and tricked me into wanting to sleep with you, which was better than raping me, I guess. Thanks for that. And I did have a lovely time, and I won't mind sleeping with you, I'm sure, ever. But I have to keep in mind that it's not a choice. I have to do whatever you tell me because I'm a slave."

Finally she stopped, having run out of thoughts. Mikael stared at her.

"What?" she said. "I'm only trying to keep my feet on the ground, you know? Be sensible. Smart. I shouldn't be dreaming about things I can't have."

"What do you want that you can't have, Lyz?" he asked, his blue eyes looking right through her.

She shook her head.

"I would like to ask you not to call me that because you should only call people sweet names if you care about them. And if this were anything like a normal situation, I would say that. But it's not a typical situation, and that's what I meant. I need to get used to the fact that you own me. And you can call me whatever you like."

She took out a tiny handkerchief from the pocket of her blouse and dabbed at her eyes, trying not to ruin her makeup. She wasn't crying anymore, but the tears from earlier were making everything muddy.

"Why does a wealthy, modern planet like Marka even have slaves?" Lyzette asked, forgetting that slaves probably shouldn't ask questions like that of their masters. "Even on Earth, which is so backward compared to Marka, it's illegal."

Mikael looked at her unhappily.

"I'm sorry. I'm talking too much. I'll shut up now," she said, turning to look out of the carriage again.

After a few minutes, Mikael spoke, and she turned so she could see him out of the corner of her eye.

"All the responses in my head sound false when I start to speak them," he said. "I was going to say that there aren't many slaves, usually only consorts. And I was going to say that we don't enslave Markans — only people from other planets."

He trailed off.

"Those excuses sounded fine before, but they don't make much sense when you're in front of me."

Lyzette looked up at him as he continued.

"Those explanations don't make any sense at all. Why is it okay to have slaves, as long as there aren't too many? Why is it okay because they're only consorts? Why is it okay because we don't enslave our people?"

He shook his head and looked out of the carriage at the busy city.

"It's not okay, Lyzette."

Lyzette stared at him. She felt disappointed. For a moment, she had thought that he was going to change the social order of the planet because she had shown him a truth, but that was ridiculous. She wasn't someone who could open people's eyes and make them change. She was a nobody. She got that. She would remember it from now on.

"What is it now?" he asked.

"Nothing." She smiled brightly, remembering what her mother always suggested. If life is kicking you in the ass, put a smile on your face and ignore the pain because your pain doesn't matter.

# CHAPTER 12

The carriage pulled up to an enormous building.

"What is this place?" Lyzette asked.

"It's the stadium where the match is," Mikael said, getting out. He held out his hand to help her exit the carriage, but she ignored it and stepped down on her own onto the street. She tilted her head up, craning her neck to try and see everything she could.

"Come on." He put his hand on her back and urged her forward off the street. The next carriage was pulling up, and they needed to get out of the way.

She stepped forward purposefully in her high heels. They were lavender and matched the rest of the outfit. Lyzette liked the sharp sound of her shoes clicking on the floor. The harsh sound matched her brittle mood.

Lyzette didn't know it, but at that moment she radiated beauty and incited desire. She was gorgeous with a post-orgasmic glow lighting her from within. Her cheeks were pink, and her curvy body was on display in a short shirt and mini-skirt.

What she did know was that every male eye in the entrance was on her. She moved closer to Mikael unconsciously, flipping her dark hair back over her shoulder. She had decided to wear her hair down tonight, and now she was having second thoughts. She would be trying to keep it out of her face all evening.

"Why are they all looking at me?" she whispered to Mikael.

"Because you're beautiful," he whispered back. "And because I haven't brought a woman to a match in a long time."

She frowned and turned her head to meet his eye. He didn't say anything else but led her through the crowd and out to the seats. They walked down to field level. The building reminded her of a small football field. Mikael opened the door to a private box seat which looked luxurious and expensive.

Once they were in the box, they could see the whole field but none of the other fans could see them. She heard a lock click once they were inside.

She was trapped again.

"This is the Markanor's private box," he said. "We'll watch from here."

"I thought you were playing today," Lyzette said. She didn't care about sports right now because she was still upset.

"I am. But there are many different setups at the one match. You'll see. It'll be easier to explain once it starts," he said.

She said nothing, and Mikael needed to break the silence.

"Lyzette," he murmured, coming to her and enfolding her in his strong arms. "I wish things were different."

"But they're not," she said, trying to pull away.

"I do care about you."

"Not really," she said. "You want to fuck me. Are those two things the same for aliens?"

He blew out a frustrated breath.

"The slave system is the way things work here. All the higher level men have consorts, even if they're married. It keeps our libidos in check. When we arrived on this planet, it was next to impossible to get a woman pregnant. When we first arrived, our race was forced to have the males pleasure the females multiple times a day in order to survive. Seven days a week. Most men had seven or eight mates to get some of them pregnant."

Lyzette was shocked.

"That's right. Our bodies adjusted, producing larger and larger amounts of sperm in shorter and shorter periods of time. When the population stabilized, there wasn't any danger of us dying out any longer, and we couldn't reverse our physiological changes. In a different society, the males only have one partner, but we were stuck. A thousand years ago, our rulers declared that men should have only one official partner but if another were needed to satisfy the requirements of the body, he could take a consort."

"A man created that rule," Lyzette said.

Mikael didn't respond to her statement. "When slave traders found out about our new laws, they provided inexpensive women used for their bodies. We kept the women of Marka in the dark. And everyone was happy."

"Everyone except the slaves," Lyzette said to herself.

"You know what that means, right, Lyzette?" he said, coming over to where she stood. His voice was husky.

"What?" she said, suddenly picking up on his change in mood.

"Lots of pleasures," he whispered, his breath hot in her ear.

She shivered. She had to let him fuck her. It was her job.

"But I'm sore!"

"Don't worry. I've got it all covered. Sit down," he said, indicating one of his plush armchairs.

She sat, keeping her knees tight together, like a lady. He knelt in front of her.

"Open your legs, Lyzette," he told her.

She spread them a little bit.

"I need access," he said, taking her knees and moving them far apart. Then he moved between her legs and brought her to climax so quickly, she couldn't believe it. Apparently, neither could he.

"I've never…" he said, shaking his head. Then he picked her up as if she were as light as a feather and deposited her on a couch near the back. She was still convulsing as he rubbed something on himself and then pushed into her.

She grimaced. She had to bear it. She was a slave, and if he wanted to fuck her when she was sore, then she had to put up with it. But he didn't move right away.

"What are you doing?" she asked. She was confused.

"Letting the painkiller I put on start to work. It takes a couple minutes."

She was surprised. He was thinking of her comfort. It didn't fit with the image of the cruel slave master she had been building up in her mind.

She lay still, waiting. She realized that although she felt pain before, now she only felt tingles of excitement. She wanted to have him fill her again.

She didn't mean to beg him to move, but she was almost going to when he pulled out and then pushed back in so fast, she huffed out her breath.

"This isn't going to be slow, Lyzette. The match is starting," he said.

"Starting?" she squeaked, turning her head to see men in shorts and no shirts running out onto the field. "What if they can see us?" But he didn't answer, focused only on plunging into her body over and over.

It was his right to fuck her in front of whoever he wanted, she supposed. She lay back ready to endure it, but in no time she was near the edge again. He dropped his hand down and rubbed her clit in tiny, light circles.

"Lyzette, I can't wait," he said, exploding inside of her. He sucked hard on her nipple, and the combination sent a shattering climax ripping through her body. She looked up and saw that one man on the field was at the correct angle to see them.

He was looking in their direction.

"Mik, get off me. Someone's watching," she said, unable to stop her hips from bucking. He turned quickly.

"No one should be able to see in, Lyzette," he said, glancing at the players lining up.

By the time he looked, the man was gone.

Lyzette felt conflicted. She was upset with Mikael for being her master. But he kept making her feel fantastic. She couldn't make up her mind about him. He thought of her comfort...in order to have more sex with her. Still, he could have fucked her and not worried about how she felt.

She was confused. Now he was trying to tell her about how this stupid match thing worked, and she didn't care, and it would be more confusing. Her body was so relaxed that she could hardly sit upright. Even though she had finished having sex only moments before, sitting beside Mikael was making her want him again.

It was all so frustrating and strange. All in all, it was looking to be an annoying afternoon.

When Mikael took the field, she forgot everything else.

He explained how the game worked earlier, but there were a lot of rules. All she had got out of it was that they had to push the other guy over the line, and certain things weren't allowed. It had something to do with keeping his clan on top. Every match was important. They needed to gain points every time to ensure they stayed in power. Blah blah blah. Even on another planet she couldn't escape men's obsessions with sports.

She watched, rapt with attention, as he squared off with the other men from his clan. She admitted that he looked dominant. They were all fine specimens, but she had eyes for no one but Mik. Although Lyzette had seen Mikael's chest for a few moments while they had played cards, she suddenly realized that she hadn't been able to see anything last night. Nothing she could appreciate. When they had made love today, both times he had kept his shirt on.

The shirt was off now, and Mikael was built. Like, tons of muscles. His biceps were large, and his chest was broad and powerful. She remembered the feel of the muscled flesh under her hands and mouth last night but to see his strength was something else entirely. His hips were narrow and his buttocks tight. In those cute shorts, she could see his lean, long legs. His rock-hard body was on display, except for the shorts. She wondered if she still had any of the venom in her that was making her so horny.

No. Raimey said that would have worn off days ago. That could only mean one thing. Even though he had taken her only minutes before, she was getting aroused again by looking at him.

The men on the field were lined up against each other and squaring off. When a whistle blew, they charged at each other. They met at the yellow line in the middle of the field and then they grappled, each man trying to push his partner across the line.

Despite her initial lack of enthusiasm, Lyzette cheered along with the crowd, rooting for Mikael's clan. Then she saw the man that watched them having sex. He lined up against Mikael. He turned his head and looked right at her again. He gave her a nasty smile. The whistle blew, and the two men wrestled back and forth over the line.

Mikael had a look of determination on his face, and he pushed hard until the other man was on the other side of the line. He kept pushing until the man lost his footing and fell. They were the last pair, and when his opponent went down, a great shout went up from the crowd.

Mikael slammed forearms with the other members of his team, which seemed to be their version of a high five - and their match was done. Lyzette watched without interest as the next two teams lined up and pushed each other around. It wasn't as much fun when you didn't know any of the participants.

She tried to sort out her muddled thoughts. She knew she liked Mikael because he was kind, funny, and unbelievably gorgeous. And of course, he was irresistibly sexy. He seemed to find her irresistible too, based on his behavior at the waterfall and here in the box. Of course, he had also explained how Markans needed to have a lot of sex.

But what about the fact that he was her master? And she was a slave? Lyzette had recognized when the alien bit her that her life was being irrevocably changed. When Mikael bought her in the slave market, she knew that was a significant shift, too.

She had expected him to be harsh and cruel, keeping her in a dungeon or something. But not this. She was living in the height of luxury, and it was better than her life as a free woman.

How was she supposed to remember that she was a slave when she was being treated better than she ever had been in her whole life?

# CHAPTER 13

Mikael put his arm around Lyzette and went along with the flow of bodies leaving the stadium. Even now, he couldn't stop thinking about when he would get to have her again.

He had never felt this way about anyone in his life before and had never wanted a woman the way he had wanted Lyzette. He had gone out of his way to please her and make sure she had her pleasure before he took his.

Of course, he hadn't asked if she was okay with fucking behind the waterfall and in the box, but she had gone with it and enjoyed it, so that was okay, wasn't it?

But what about her comments about slaves? He became uncomfortable when she referred to herself as a slave. He felt she was demeaning herself.

Was he demeaning her as well?

He owned her and paid an exorbitant sum for her at the slave market because he hadn't been able to keep his eyes off of her, even then.

And she was surprising. She made him laugh unexpectedly. She was an amazing woman, not a slave. The other slave women had been merely bodies for him to enjoy. He treated them well, but they had only been a way to blow off steam, nothing more.

Lyzette was something else entirely, and he was still learning that.

There was no reasonable way to free slaves on Marka. They left the planet, died themselves, or their masters died — that was their path to freedom.

Was it wrong that slaves couldn't be liberated? Even if it was reprehensible, there wasn't anything he could do about it. Many influential clan leaders and commoners kept consorts. The system was established and impossible to change.

Markan women were delicate and wouldn't have sex with you only because you wanted them to. But the slaves, they were required to do what the man wanted, and that was the way men liked it. It was the way he had liked it, until now.

Shouldn't the women have a choice, though? How could they claim to revere their females, then enslave women from other planets to be their living sex toys at the same time? It was the ultimate hypocrisy.

Trying to change anything would bring about his clan's downfall and allow the Delanor to rise to power and take over. That wasn't a good outcome. But he couldn't support keeping women as sex slaves either.

What was he to do?

People spilled out of the building and spread through the streets, heading home. Mikael looked around for Jol, but he couldn't find his driver.

"Jol's not here again. Perhaps he parked somewhere in the surrounding streets. I'll send him a message," he said. "Hm. He's not reading it. I wonder what's going on? We'll walk around and look for him. What do you think of that? Want to see some more of the city?"

"Is it safe?" Lyzette asked, looking around at the dark streets fearfully.

"I'm with you. You're always safe now," Mikael said, brushing aside her worry. He wasn't concerned.

"What about the man who saw us? The one you defeated at the end? What about him?" she said.

How did she know that man was the Delanor and his enemy?

"That's the Delanor. We haven't got along since I convinced his girlfriend to 'watch the matches' in my private box."

"You fucked his girlfriend?" Lyzette said, with such candidness that he was shocked. "So he hates you."

"Yes."

"I think we should wait here for Jol," she said, looking around at the brightly lit area in front of the stadium. "We could even go back inside."

"Lyzette," he said, shaking his head. "It's fine. I'm the Markanor, remember? People don't mess with me. And by extension, they won't mess with you. Got it?"

"But that man hit you today," she said.

"It's okay."

She nodded but didn't look convinced. Mikael moved quickly across the street and turned into the smaller lane that led up to the stadium. It was dimly lit but not seedy. He showed her the dining district that surrounded the stadium. There were dozens of shops with different specialties of baked goods.

"See?" Mikael said. "This shop makes only filled pastries. They're pretty good. I'll bring you here one day, and we'll get an entire box."

He stopped speaking and stood very still, listening intently.

"What is it?" Lyzette said, looking up at him and then around the street. He stood frozen a moment longer then looked down at her and smiled, tucking her into the crook of his arm.

"Nothing," he smiled confidently. "Just some people shouting."

But he didn't like what he'd heard. It was odd to hear people yelling at this time of the night, and they weren't speaking words. It sounded like a code the Delanor and his clan used to signal each other.

Why hadn't he listened when Lyzette said they should stay at the stadium?

"We should head back and call for a cab. Who knows where Jol's gone?" Or if he's tied up in a basement somewhere, he thought.

He tried not to seem rushed, but he walked them as quickly as he could back towards the main street. Lyzette held onto his hand tightly and walked as fast as her stupid shoes would let her. Why did women wear such things? Then he remembered how she had looked with her shapely calves on display as she strode into the stadium. He couldn't resist, and her calves looked and felt good. He liked it when she had them wrapped around him while he took her in his private box. She drove him crazy.

He looked down at her dark head and felt a stab of fear. It was his job to protect her. And alone in the city, with the Delanors surrounding him at this very moment, he wasn't sure if he could.

The thought frightened him.

"Lyzette, if anything should happen, I want you to take those lovely shoes off and run as fast as you can back to the stadium, okay? It's at the end of this street. It's not far at all."

"Something's going on, isn't it?" Lyzette said, her big blue eyes wide with fear. "Mikael, do you have a weapon?"

He shook his head. He hadn't thought to bring one. And it wouldn't have been allowed in the stadium. Marka was a safe place, damn it! Unless your enemy was trying for a huge point gain by beating you senseless and taking your girl. It might even be enough to shift the balance away from his clan.

"Fuck," Mikael said under his breath. Lyzette moaned, and she slipped her shoes off, clutching them in her free hand and stepping gingerly along the sidewalk in her bare feet.

The Delanor was a ruthless asshole who had his eye on Mikael's power for a long time. The fact that Mikael had been stupid enough to fuck his girlfriend had not helped things. It had only made him angrier and more resentful. Mikael honestly couldn't say what the Delanor would do. Mikael's murder was a possibility, and he quickened his step, dragging Lyzette along with him.

His heart was pounding. Three more blocks. Maybe there wasn't anything to worry about after all, but his senses were on high alert.

In the end, his enemies attacked from the rooftops.

"Run, Lyz," he cried, pushing her towards the stadium. She took off, and he turned to face his first opponent. He recognized him. He fought so often with the Delanor's clan they were as familiar to him as his own.

He backed away as the man came at him with wild, swinging punches. Mikael ducked once, then twice and came up underneath with a solid blow to the solar plexus. He knocked his assailant back onto his butt.

Mikael whirled around as the next one attacked. He caught Mikael's chin and knocked him off balance a bit, but not enough to stop his forward momentum. Mikael tackled him and punched him hard in the face, ensuring that he would stay down for awhile. The first guy was still sitting on the ground. He had the wind knocked out of him.

Two men came to him next. He swung at one and hit him, but the other man landed four or five quick punches to the gut, bending Mikael over. As the first thug recovered, he sent a vicious hook flying into Mikael's ear, which started ringing. But he didn't go down.

The two attacked at once, and he had a hard time defending against four sets of hands. He took several hits to the face, and he felt his lip split. He probably had a black eye, but he was coming out okay. He could handle two.

Just then seven or eight more men stepped out of the shadows. Mikael knew that they wouldn't attack. The first four had been a warning.

When the Delanor walked out into the middle of the street, he knew that things had gone from bad to worse.

He glanced up towards the stadium and hoped that Lyzette was safe inside.

"Well, well, well," said the Delanor. The voice made Mikael want to vomit. "Hello, Markanor. You're looking well tonight. Probably because you were shagging your new slave rotten at the match."

The men all laughed. Mikael tightened his jaw. The Delanor had the upper hand.

"You did well against my men, but I think even you might find twelve well-trained soldiers overwhelming."

Mikael said nothing. The Delanor would get to the point when he damn well felt like it.

"If I sic them on you, you might find yourself beaten to a pulp in the hospital the next time you wake up. Who would defend your new slave then?" he asked.

Hadn't Lyzette made it to the stadium already?

"But I won't need to do that, will I? You're going to cooperate. Sometimes street fights go badly, and people end up dead, even Markanors or their consorts."

He was threatening murder. Okay. Mikael could deal. Then he would figure out a way to take this man out once and for all.

"I'll cooperate. What do you want, Deese?"

"Such a good boy, aren't you, Mikael? You always have been. But it's bad form to fuck a woman where anyone can see it. It makes men want things they shouldn't have."

Deese had seen when he'd taken Lyzette in the box. That's the man she had noticed. Where was this going?

Just then, a man pulled Lyzette out where Mikael could see her. The man had tied her arms behind her, and she had a gag in her mouth. She looked beautiful and terrified. He trembled. He wanted to protect her but knew that any move on his part might get himself incapacitated or hurt her.

"It makes men want to take women that aren't theirs," Deese said, and he smiled. The smile radiated pure triumph. That's when it clicked for Mikael. This abduction was about Deese's revenge. He hadn't gotten over Mikael fucking his girlfriend, never mind that she had been willing. Deese had been biding his time.

Deese couldn't have picked a better person to use against him. Mikael realized that when he had said that he cared for Lyzette, it was because he had feelings in his soul. Now Deese had her, and he didn't know what he was going to do to her.

"I'll return her when I feel like it, Mikael," Deese said, walking over to Lyzette and twisting her nipple. It was standing out against the thin fabric. She looked angry and made a sound against her gag. "Mmmm, feisty. Just the way I like my women."

Mikael breathed heavily, and his hands clenched and unclenched into fists. He shook and felt like fighting. He forced himself to hold back, knowing anything he did would make the situation worse.

"You know where to take him," Deese said. Two men came up to Mikael and secured his hands behind his back. "As for the slave girl?"

He stopped, making sure that he looked Mikael straight in the eyes.

"Put her in my bed."

# CHAPTER 14

They tied Mikael to a chair in front of a viewscreen and left him alone in the room. He worked to loosen the ropes trapping him on the chair. Had the men given any slack at all to work with? He felt desperate knowing that Lyzette was at Deese's mercy.

He had failed to protect her. It was as devastating as any other failure in his life. In the back of his mind, he knew the points he lost would result in a massive loss of power.

Of course, he had also been beaten up and kidnapped. The twin failures could be enough to shift the balance to the Delanor clan.

He worked away at the ropes. They were tight, but he had big wrists. If he loosened his bonds enough, his hands could slip through. As a boy, his older brothers had tied him up and left him for hours. The key to getting free was patience and believing the knot could be undone.

He wondered if Lyz was okay. He tried not to think about what was happening to her in Deese's bed. It made his blood boil to think of anyone else having her.

She was his.

But more than that, he didn't want any harm to come to her. He needed her.

The realization slapped him in the face and motivated
him to get out of there and save her, patience be damned.
He wiggled and shook, feeling the rope on his right wrist
getting nearly loose enough for his hand to slip through.

Just then, Deese walked in.

"Mikael," he said, smiling charmingly. "I came to have a
talk with you before I go to bed."

He stood before Mikael.

"She's beautiful, your new little slave. By the look on her
face earlier tonight, she enjoys being fucked," he said,
watching for Mikael's reaction.

He cursed himself again for being stupid enough to take
her in public, twice. The first time had been lucky. The
second time he had been dumb. He'd gotten carried
away, and now they were paying for it.

"She'll beg me not to fuck her, but I won't listen. These
women don't care who the cock inside them belongs to,
as long as it's big."

"So she's going to care, is that what you're trying to tell
me?" Mikael asked.

Deese pressed his lips together but continued his victory
speech.

"She's going to be mine, Mikael," he said. "And you're
going to watch, because imagining what I'm doing to her
won't inflict enough pain on you. You're going to pay for

taking Meessla from me. You will have to watch me take your new little favorite fuck over and over and over," he whispered.

He had a triumphant look on his face as he switched on the viewscreen. It showed Lyzette tied to a massive bed. She only had on her underwear, and she looked terrified. Mikael's heart squeezed in his chest.

"See the little beauty. I'm sure she's wet for me. She can't wait to be taken by a real man," Deese was going on, but Mikael wasn't listening. He had gone back to work on the ropes holding him and was trying to look like he wasn't getting himself untied. He had to get Lyzette away from this madman. "This camera will give you the perfect view of us."

He trailed off as he watched one of his men enter the room. Deese frowned.

"He's not supposed to be in there."

They watched as he moved towards the bed. Deese and Mikael could hear the noises from the bedroom through the viewscreen.

"If you weren't the Delanor's, I would fuck your brains out, slave," he said, rubbing her between the legs.

Mikael felt rage building inside him. Did the Delanor have any control over his men?

"I bet you're wet, waiting to be fucked by the Delanor, huh? You little whores like it no matter who's in your cunt."

The man looked around and did something to the camera. The viewscreen went dark.

"That fucker," Deese said and bolted from the room, his face a mask of fury.

Then the camera came back on. The man had probably tried to turn it off, not knowing that Deese had a unique security system. The cameras could never be deactivated. That was part of Deese's torture plan for Mikael - as he saw Deese have his way with Lyzette, there would be no way for Mikael to stop watching.

He tried to tune out what the man was saying, but saw him get on the bed and pull her legs apart.

Mikael struggled with the ropes, then made himself calm down. If he pulled too hard, he would make them tighter.

He tried to keep his eyes off the screen, but he couldn't seem to look away. He watched, feeling nauseated as the man bent and sucked on one of Lyzette's breasts. She kicked and struggled, trying to get away from him.

Mikael was dying inside thinking about that pig. His sweet little Lyzette, who had responded so beautifully last night. She had given herself to him for the first time and came so quickly. To think that such a sexual being could have that spoiled by an asshole out for revenge against him made him sick.

The situation was all his fault. He had got sloppy and made stupid mistakes, playing right into his enemy's hands.

On the screen, the man was touching her between her legs.

"Oh, you like that do you?" he said, and he was lining himself to enter. "Wait until I get my cock up in your pussy."

Mikael twisted his wrists desperately and felt the ropes cut through his raw skin. When he pulled and strained long enough, he was able to get one hand out. He grimaced when he looked at the bloody mess of his wrist, but ignored the pain and went to work on the other one.

Mikael looked up when he heard Deese's voice. Oh, thank goodness, he stopped the man before he could have his way with her. The Delanor was furious and was taking the man out of the room. If Mikael knew Deese at all, the man would be shot.

Mikael tried and tried, but he couldn't get the ropes on the other wrist loose at all and eventually got free by scraping enough skin off so he could rip himself out.

He looked at the screen to see what was happening now. The situation hadn't improved. It incensed him to see Deese sliding his hand into Lyzette's folds.

"You're wet," he said in surprise. "Maybe you're not as unwilling as I thought you would be. That won't do."

Then he drew back and slapped her hard across the face. Mikael didn't waste any more time.

He made a noise to draw the guard into the room, then hid against the wall so the guard wouldn't be able to see him. When the guard opened the door to investigate, Mikael jumped him. He attacked with all the vicious force from his feelings of powerlessness.

"Where is he keeping her?" he said. The young man had collapsed on the floor and held his stomach.

The guard was bleeding and nearly unconscious, but Mikael grabbed him by the head and forced the guard to look at him.

"Where. Is. She? Tell me, or you're dead."

Mikael wasn't sure if he would kill, but the more he thought about Lyzette at the mercy of his enemy, the more he felt like he was capable of anything. It wasn't an idle threat.

The young man thought about his best interests, and he gave Mikael directions to the Delanor.

The Markanor punched him hard one more time, knocking him unconscious. He ducked out the door and locked the guard inside.

Mikael pitied the young man. When his superiors found out he let the prisoner escape, he was going to be in trouble. Then he took off down the dark corridor, thinking of no one but Lyz.

# CHAPTER 15

Lyzette was petrified. She was wearing only her bra and a thong. Her wrists were tied tightly to the bedposts on the Delanor's bed. They had put a new gag in her mouth.

She wondered how things had gone from good to bad so quickly. It was like her mother always said: "When something good happens, look around because pretty soon the other shoe will drop."

She pulled at her bonds and wished they weren't tight. Of course, what would she do even if she got loose? They blindfolded her on the way here so that she had no idea where she was going. There were no windows in this room, so she supposed they were in a subterranean hideout. Didn't villains always have underground lairs?

A man walked in and looked at her.

"Oh boy," he said, moving towards the bed. "If you weren't the Delanor's, I would fuck your brains out, slave."

He put his hand between her legs and rubbed her through the cloth.

"I bet you're wet, waiting to be fucked by the Delanor, huh? You little whores like it no matter who's in your cunt."

He looked around furtively and then he went to the wall and pressed a button.

"Now there will be no record. He won't be along for another hour. The Delanor likes his baths after a match," he said, unbuckling his pants.

Lyzette's eyes grew wide with horror when she saw his cock spring free. He climbed onto the bed. She had her legs tightly squeezed together, but he pried them apart. Once he was between her legs, he pulled one of her breasts out and sucked it a moment. She made an angry sound and struggled.

"Don't pretend you don't like it," he said, leering at her. "The Delanor wasn't the only one who got a look at you and Mikael in his public box."

He pulled the thong aside and slid his hand into her folds. She made another infuriated noise and pulled on the silk ribbons that held her prisoner, trying to twist her body away from him.

"Oh, you like that do you?" he said, and she felt his hardness brush her sex. "Well, wait until I get my cock up in there."

Click.

They both looked up and were surprised to see the Delanor holding a gun to the man's head. The man froze in the act of penetrating her.

"Deese, I swear I wasn't going to do anything. I was getting her ready for you. You can imagine how tight she is."

"Get up and put your prick back in your pants. You'll be lucky if I let you keep either your cock or your miserable life," the Delanor said coldly. He was furious. "If there weren't a lady present, I would blow your brains out right now. Men who can't follow orders become Clanless or dead quickly."

"I can follow orders sir, I swear. Punish me, whip me, do whatever you want to me. But don't declan me, sir, please," the man was begging now. He was frightened out of his mind.

Lyzette remembered how Mikael had said that you either had a clan, or you left the planet.

"Come with me," the Delanor said. He kept the gun pressed against the man's head and the two men left the room.

Lyzette squirmed around trying to get her thong back into position, but she couldn't get her breast back in her bra — that was impossible.

The waiting was horrible. She remembered how bad Mikael had looked the last time she had seen him in the street, with a bloody lip and a black eye. There was a bruise on his cheek too, and he had been holding his side like it hurt.

What if the Delanor killed him?

The thought of the Delanor made her break out in a cold sweat. What was he going to do to her? He meant to have his way with her in revenge for what Mikael had done to his girlfriend. But she had no idea if he would hurt her or beat her or even kill her when his vengeance was complete. She was scared out of her mind.

The only sex she had before was with Mikael. She realized that she wasn't a slut because if she were, she would be excited to sleep with this guy too.

She wasn't. She didn't want him anywhere near her. Her revulsion made her feel a tiny bit better, but not much. She was going to get raped, and there wasn't anything she could do about it.

She tried desperately to think about how she could protect her mind from what was about to happen. The only thing she could do was think of Mikael, about how he had touched her and how she had enjoyed it. She pretended that it was him coming to her now and that he would be filling her.

That only worked for a second. She knew it wouldn't be Mikael, since he was locked up somewhere, being beaten or killed. No one would come to her aid. Just like in the alleyway, the men only wanted her for one thing.

She clenched her thighs tightly together and waited, trying to think of nothing and feeling fear coursing through her body. She was in big trouble, and there was no escape this time.

The Delanor strode back into the room by himself. He stood and looked her over, then roughly shoved her breast into her bra. Stepping back, he crossed his arms over his chest and surveyed her again.

Lyzette blushed as he gazed at her nearly naked body. He came over again and undid her gag. She spat it out gratefully. When he offered her a drink of water, she took it.

He moved away yet again and she tried to calm the tremors in her body, as she attempted to figure out what he was up to. That's when she realized he wanted her to be frightened. He wanted her to be as negatively affected by this experience as possible so he could hurt Mikael.

Finally he moved towards her and with a deft flick of one hand, he undid the clasp on her bra. Damn Raimey for insisting on the front clasp.

Her plump breasts burst free, and he drew in a breath. Lyzette clenched her teeth together. How long was he going to take? Couldn't he just rape her and be done with it?

He reached out and fondled one breast, and her traitorous nipple beaded tightly from his touch. His eyes darted to hers, and she narrowed them at him, refusing to give him the pleasure of struggling or making any sound, no matter how disgusted she was.

He bent over and took her breast between his teeth, watching her all the time. She did her best to keep still and not try to flee from the bastard. How could she stop him? She had her legs free. Maybe she could knee him? Then he would hurt her as well as rape her. She had never tried to change the course of events in her life before, and it didn't make much sense to start now.

When he snaked his hand down to her thong, she damned Raimey again for making it so easy for these fucking men to touch her. He pushed it aside as if it were nothing and slid his finger into her folds. She was still wet from when Mikael had made love to her at the match, but he wouldn't know that. He would think she was wet for him, the fucker. She was angry. She was ready to explode, but she couldn't do anything.

"You're wet," he said in surprise. "Maybe you're not as unwilling as I thought you would be. That won't do," he said.

He brought his arm back and slapped her hard across the face. Her face was expressionless, and she didn't cry out even though she wanted to.

"Damn you, girl. Not even a whimper? I wanted you to beg me not to fuck you. Beg me, damn it!"

She stared at him steadily.

He was enraged. Then he got a wild glint in his eyes.

"If you don't beg me, I'll kill Mikael," he said.

She looked at him, wondering if he was serious. She couldn't take a chance that he might kill Mikael simply because she wasn't doing what she was supposed to. If begging meant that she would save his life, she would do it.

"Please don't touch me," she said.

"That wasn't very convincing," he said, frowning and playing idly with one of her nipples.

"Leave me the fuck alone," she said, letting some of her rage out.

He smiled then, and she wished he hadn't.

"That's more like it," he said, stroking her rigid buds with both hands. It was a physiological reaction. She couldn't help it. She didn't want the asshole to touch her.

Then he pinched both of them hard.

"Ow," she said. She was getting angrier.

"Beg me," he ordered. "More desperate, less angry."

Now he was giving her acting lessons? What the fuck was up with this guy?

"Please leave me alone," she said in her most desperate voice, and it wasn't acting.

"No," he said, getting off the bed and dropping his pants. "You want me to fuck you, I'm going to, and you're going to love it."

"No," she said, trying to twist away. He was going to do it. He had lulled into complacency, but now she was terrified.

"No!" she screamed as he pulled off her thong, leaving her sex completely vulnerable to his assault and wrenching her legs apart.

He knelt between her thighs, taking himself in hand and she felt his cock touch her entrance. Unable to help herself, she screamed.

"Yeah, that's right, baby, cry out," he said.

At the moment when Lyzette thought rape was inevitable, he suddenly keeled over, collapsing on the bed. She looked around. What had happened? Did he have a heart attack?

"Stun gun, lethal setting," Mikael said, walking over and pushing the dead body off the bed where it landed with a thump. Then he turned to Lyzette with concern in his eyes. "Are you okay?"

Lyzette nodded dumbly. Raimey walked over, pulling a knife from her pocket and snapping the blade out. She cut the bonds that held Lyzette captive.

"When Jol couldn't find you two, we suspected some foul play," she explained. "And since everyone knows where Deese's underground lair is, we came over."

"All of you?" Lyzette said.

"Sure? What else did we have to do? I shot three guys tonight. Sure beats shelling peas," she said. Raimey smiled at Lyzette.

Mikael helped Lyzette scramble off the bed. Her legs were shaking. She was reeling from the fact that she had almost been raped — twice. She was also trying to come to terms with the idea that Raimey and the others had helped to save her. She was wrong about them being jealous.

Lyzette pulled on her thong and skirt. Her shirt was nowhere to be seen but at least she had her bra.

She crossed her arms over her chest and felt like throwing up.

"Ready?" Mikael said. When Lyzette nodded, he led the way out, leaving Deese's dead body on the floor.

# CHAPTER 16

Lyzette curled up in her bed the next morning. She didn't want to get up and face the day. She was lucky that she had escaped without being raped, but she was feeling traumatized by her situation.

She locked her door and wasn't letting anyone in, no matter how much the women knocked and pleaded. They went away eventually. Mikael hadn't shown up yet, but she wouldn't be able to turn him away.

She didn't want to face anyone. She felt dirty.

She couldn't help replaying certain moments in her mind.

She didn't know if she would ever like sex again, or if she'd be able to have sex with Mikael. She longed for him, but not in a sexual way. She wanted to feel safe. That was all, and nothing more.

There couldn't be anything more between a slave and her master.

She closed her eyes and tried to go to sleep when suddenly she heard a thump on her balcony. She sat up in bed. She was wearing a pair of long pajamas which covered as much of her body as possible. She didn't want to see herself.

Mikael's head peeked in through one of the French doors a moment later, and her heart stopped pounding.

"Mikael," she said, lying back down. She turned away from him and pulled the covers up, curling into a ball.

"Lyzette, I know that you didn't want to see anyone."

"But you're my master, and you have access to me anytime you want. I know," she said, her voice dull. She wondered if he wanted her body right now. Why else would he come? She sat up then and began unbuttoning her pajama top.

"What are you doing?" Mikael asked, looking confused.

"Don't you want me?" she said, and it was her turn to look confused.

"Right now? For sex? Are you crazy? Of course not, especially not after what happened yesterday."

Lyzette stopped unbuttoning.

"I was going to say that I know you didn't want to see anyone, but I had to make sure you were okay. And I wanted to apologize."

"Apologize? But you didn't do anything wrong."

"I did. I committed the ultimate sin. I didn't protect a woman in my care. And for that I am sorry, Lyzette. I should have done better."

"You saved me in the end," she said, staring at him.

"It never should have happened. I got sloppy. I made mistakes, and Deese took advantage of me. It should never have happened," he repeated. "Please forgive me."

"There's nothing to forgive," she said, stunned. No one had ever apologized to her before and asked her forgiveness. She had thought that was all fiction in books she was forced to read in school.

He walked over and sat down on the bed, wrapping his strong arms around her. She held onto him and sighed deeply. She felt the sobs rising inside of her. She tried to stop them, but she couldn't. They were too powerful and overwhelmed her.

She cried and cried. Mikael held her and offered her a tissue to blow her nose.

"Mikael, you don't understand. Things like that happen to girls like me all the time. It's probably all my fault. That's what mother said whenever anything bad happened to me."

Mikael stared at her, shaking his head.

"Pardon my swearing, Lyz, but your mother sounds like a real bitch. Nothing that happened to you last night was your fault. If it was anyone's fault, it was mine. And you're not to believe such nonsense anymore. I think you should forget everything your mother ever told you."

"Maybe," Lyzette said. "She didn't like me very much."

She started crying again. It wasn't because she missed her mother, but because she didn't miss her at all, which seemed inappropriate. They sat holding hands side by side on the bed. Eventually, Lyzette looked down at their clasped hands and frowned at the bandages on Mikael's wrists.

She looked carefully at his face. It was difficult to see. Dim light filtered into her room through her closed curtains. She saw a black eye and purple bruise on his cheek, and a cut lip.

"Mikael, you're hurt," she said, running her fingers lightly along his cheek where the bruise was.

"It's nothing. I would have gladly gotten hurt more if I could have prevented what happened to you last night."

She sniffed and sighed.

"What happened to your wrists?" she asked.

"I was tied up. I had to get away. I did whatever I needed to do to get free. It was not a choice to remain a prisoner anymore."

She lay down again.

"Mikael, will you hold me?" she whispered. She was afraid he would leave and afraid he wouldn't want to touch her if there wasn't sex involved.

"Of course, Lyzzie," he said, lying down behind her and wrapping his arm around her, pulling her tight against his body. "You're safe now. And I swear I won't ever let anything happen to you again."

---

Life returned to normal the next day, and Lyzette came out of her room. No one gave her special treatment. Mikael had told everyone she didn't want people coddling her.

She helped in the kitchen and washed more windows. She tried to put it all behind her.

But there was the issue of having sex again. She didn't know what to do about that. It seemed strange that something she had never done before should become central to her life so quickly. But she supposed that was the life of a consort. It was all about sex.

That night at supper, the women were talking about the latest gossip — the shifts in the clans.

"The Markanor lost us a shitload of points two days ago," Delia said, not looking at Lyzette. "And The Delanor is taking advantage of it. He's attacked all nine of the other clans in the past two days, earning points from all of them. He won't need to win by much at the match tonight."

She looked grim at the thought.

"I thought the Delanor was dead," Lyzette said. She suddenly felt frightened.

"I mean his replacement, sweetie, don't worry," Delia said, patting Lyzette's hand.

"I don't understand," Lyzette said.

"Their clan is nearly equal to ours for points by now. By taking so many points in such a short period, his clan will only need to win three of their setups to surpass our clan."

"But doesn't that mean that they will usurp the Markanor?"

"That's right, Lyzzie. The ruler hasn't been taken out like this in over a hundred years. Usually, the person dies, and the clans battle it out to see who comes out on top. These sorts of machinations aren't the Markan way, dear," Maureen said.

"What will happen to us?" Lyzette asked, feeling small and helpless.

"The Markanor wouldn't be ruling the planet anymore, so he would become the Hawthanor again, like before their family came into power. But there won't be a large difference in his wealth."

"Oh," she said, the relief pouring through her. If Maureen told her that someone else was going to buy her, she would have died right then and there. She couldn't stand all the turmoil and fear again. She wasn't strong enough. Lyzette didn't even know how she had made it this far.

A part of herself was intensely glad that she would still be with Mikael. She squashed that thought, but now that it had emerged, she couldn't unthink it.

"But what about Mikael?" She didn't know how he would feel, but she was sure he wouldn't be happy.

"You mean, the Markanor, Lyzette," Maureen reproved her sharply. "He doesn't like slaves calling him by his given name."

"He doesn't?" Lyzette wondered. She was confused. He had told her to call him Mikael.

"Never. It's simply not done, my dear. Now I don't know how you heard his name but don't ever say it again. Slaves don't call their masters by name."

Lyzette jaw hung open, and she shut her mouth.

"You understand, Lyzzie?" Maureen said. "I'm sorry to speak sharply, but I don't want you to get into trouble, dear. Okay?"

Lyzette nodded. From what Maureen had said, she committed a gross breach of etiquette. But Mikael had told her to call him by his name, right? What did that mean?

The only thing she could imagine was that he didn't consider her a slave. Why would that be, she didn't know, but it troubled and confused her. Did Mikael have feelings for her that were more than sexual? She didn't know. But she wanted to find out.

* * *

Mikael walked back into the compound and up to the house. He ambled around, doing an inspection out of habit, as his father had always done when he returned home after a trip away. Mikael had only been in the city for a day, meeting with the advisors of his clan.

He noticed some gutters that needed cleaning and a window frame to repaint. When he got to the back of the house, he realized that somehow his meandering path had brought him directly underneath Lyz's bedroom. He couldn't keep himself from glancing up at her balcony. He hoped but did not expect to see her.

She was there.

Her long dark hair was down around her face, and she wore a pure white nightgown. He thought he could make out her dark nipples but perhaps it was only his imagination.

He longed to have her again and make love to her, but he didn't know what to do. She didn't want her to touch him, and he wouldn't impose. He didn't mean to push her into anything.

How long could he contain his desire for her?
She held a notebook in her hand and gazed at the moons, sketching furiously. She would draw for a few moments, then look back up at the sky and sketch some more. She was absorbed in her work.

He hadn't known she was an artist, and he wondered what other secrets she had. He wanted to know everything. How she liked her coffee. Whether she wore socks to bed in the winter time. And most of all, what he wanted to know was how she felt about him.

He sighed.

His father had raised him to be a man's man and to win at the matches. He knew how to fight hard. He worked out, and his body looked good. No fat, lots of muscles.

But this scrap of a girl from some backwater, no-name planet, had him watching her in the moonlight and sighing. What was wrong with him?

And that's when it hit him, like a surprise push in a match that landed you on your ass.

He loved her.

This little slave that he could never marry. She seemed to be afraid of her own shadow. She barely valued herself higher than a piece of trash. This beautiful woman had given her virginity to him with such passion that it took his breath away.

He loved her.

He, the Markanor of the entire planet, loved a slave. It wouldn't do. It wouldn't do at all. Now that he could see it, there was no denying his feelings.

He loved Lyzette, but she was his slave. He could possess her body, but he could never have her as his wife, and that was the only thing he wanted.

# CHAPTER 17

"Lyzette, you don't have to come to the match if you don't want to," Mikael said. He sat down next to her in the orchard.

She had started coming out here after her work was done, to draw. Her sketch pad was hidden behind her back as she leaned against the tree. The instinct to conceal it was too powerful for her to stop now.

He took her hand but didn't try to kiss her. He hadn't attempted anything since that night.

Lyzette didn't know if she was glad or sorry.

"The match? When?"

"It's tonight. I thought you knew. It's the final match. The one that will decide everything."

"Your clan could lose, and then you wouldn't be the ruler of the planet anymore."

"That's right."

"Would you be upset if that happened?" she asked.

"Not for me, but for my clan. I would be letting them down."

He drew in a deep breath and let it out.

"It might be nice personally to have that burden lifted from my shoulders. But when I think that the Delanors would be the ruling clan, I know it would be a very, very bad idea. I can't lose tonight, Lyzette."

"I'm sure you won't," she said, squeezing his hand. "But what happens if you do?"

"I forfeit the crown right then and there. Unless the man who wins takes the trade. There's an ancient tradition that if the man who wins doesn't want to rule, he can ask the ruler for anything."

"Anything? Like he could take your entire fortune?" she said. A rule like that seemed unbelievable.

"Yes, everything I own."

"Weird."

"But nobody ever takes it. I don't know why we don't get rid of the rule. It's silly. Who would accept the trade instead of the crown?"

"Yeah," she said, staring at their hands and wishing he would touch her again. Maybe he thought she was tainted now because the hands of those men had been on her body. Maybe he found the idea of caressing her vile now. Maybe he would get a new consort.

The thought hurt her, but she ignored the pain. What she wanted wasn't important. She was so caught up in her thoughts that she missed it when he asked the question the first time. Mikael had to repeat himself.

"Why are you hiding that book behind your back?" he said, casually.

"You know?" she said. Shit. No one could know. It was her only secret. Her only love. Drawing was the only thing that made her happy. She couldn't have people laughing at it and spoiling it. She hadn't been quick enough to put it away, and he had seen her.

"Lyzette."

"It's mine." Then she remembered that he was her master, and he had asked her about the book. Did she possess anything that was her own? With dread in her heart, she pulled it out and handed it to him.

"Can I look at it?" he asked.

She nodded, not meeting his eye, feeling sick to her stomach. He opened it and began turning the pages. There were drawings from home and new ones at the end that showed her time on Marka.

"Is this what Earth looks like?"

"Some places," she said, waiting for him to laugh at the drawings.

"Wow, this is great!"

She snuck a look at him when he said that. His eyes were wide with amazement. He turned his head to look at her.

"These are beautiful, Lyzzie. You didn't tell me you were an artist."

She laughed, then, a mirthless self-mocking sound.

"Oh God, Mikael. I'm not an artist."

There was a look of disbelief on his face.

"Have you even looked at these drawings? The beauty, the feelings that you've captured? Lyzette, if you aren't an artist, I don't know what an artist is."

She frowned. What did he mean?

"They're just some sketches. I do it because I like to. Not because I'm good."

"Well, that may have been true before, but it's not now. You're the real deal, girl. I've seen some good stuff, and I know that this is quality."

She looked at him, confusion reigning in her heart and mind. Was he lying? Was he telling the truth? Why would he say such things to her when he could have said they were terrible?

Then she realized that Mikael was not her mother, and he would not treat her the way her mother would. She would have laughed at her and told her how horrible they were until she had destroyed every scrap of joy Lyzette had ever got from drawing.

He handed the book back to her. She held it to her chest, wrapping her arms around it protectively.

"Again, you don't have to come with me. That's why I wanted to find you. I didn't want you to feel that you had to come to the match."

"No, I want to go with you," Lyzette said in a firm voice. It was a tone she had never heard come from her mouth before.

"You do?" He seemed surprised as well.

"Yes. I want to be there for if you need me for anything."

"You are willing to go back to the stadium where all this started?"

She nodded decisively, ignoring the curl of fear that twisted in her guts.

"Are you sure, Lyzette?" he said.

"Yes."

"But why?" She shrugged. She didn't understand why herself. She only knew that if he were going to have to do something hard, she would want to be there if he needed her help.

"Okay. We'll leave at six o'clock."

---

Lyzette stepped out of the carriage. She grabbed Mikael's hand this time and looked around her. There were people everywhere, and she felt naked, exposed, and vulnerable.

She looked at Mikael and smiled bravely. She didn't feel her best, but her mother always said that the shittier you felt, the better you ought to look. The compliments would make you feel better, and you wouldn't feel so awful.

Lyzette was wearing a long, clingy royal blue gown that hugged her curves all the way to her toes. There was a long slit up to her hips that flashed a tantalizing glimpse of her leg as she walked. It was all held up with spaghetti straps that were so thin an observer would wonder if the whole thing was going to fall off.

She had her hair done in a French twist and on her feet she wore her favorite type of shoes - high heel. No matter the outfit, she always felt that heels were the appropriate shoe to go with it. Heels gave you stature — both height and status. She knew she looked good, and men's heads were turning as she walked past.

When she spotted her reflection in the doors to the stadium, she was shocked. She and Mikael looked good. Like they belonged together.

Like a couple.

Lyzette had never been a part of a couple. Technically, she wasn't sure if it was possible for a master and slave to be a pair. But they looked like one. She imagined the other women present wished they could on Mikael's arm, just like her.

It was strange. She had never been the object of envy before.

"Come on," he murmured in her ear. They made their way to his private box, and he opened the door for her. "I promise not to jump you this time."

She smiled at his joke but felt a sting in her heart. He wouldn't make love to her in the box. She knew that. He hadn't touched her in days. She wasn't sure if she was his consort anymore. But tonight was not the time for that discussion. She was here to support him in a sporting event that would determine their futures.

The matches began, and they sat side by side in comfortable chairs watching without much interest. They were waiting for the main event. When it was time for Mikael to get dressed, she stood up.

"Good luck," she said. She stood on tiptoe and kissed him on the cheek.

"Thanks, Lyz," he said, reaching out to run the back of his hand along the side of her face. He sighed. "I have to go."

"I'll see you after," she said.

He seemed reluctant to leave. "I don't want to leave you here alone. I should have thought of that. Jol could have come to accompany you."

"I'll be fine, Mikael, don't worry," Lyzette said. "I'll lock the door after you leave. No one can get in. You worry about the match."

Finally, he left. She saw him running out onto the field, displaying his beautiful chest. She wished things were like they were before, before that night when everything had changed.

The matches went quickly and soon they were down to the last three setups between the Markanor's clan and the Delanor's. Lyzette understood the sport enough now to see when a setup was going to go to Mikael's team or the others. A little twitch here or a step back there would show someone was going to lose.

Mikael didn't lose any. Soon it was down to the last setup and the last pair. The clans were tied, and this would decide their fate. Mikael faced off against a burly man from the Delanor's clan. She didn't see how he could win. They had pitted him against someone bigger and stronger on purpose.

The whistle blew, and they began pushing each other. The man shoved Mikael across his line and Mikael pushed him back. The crowd was silent and tense as they watched history being made. In the future, they'd be able to tell their grandchildren they were present at a historic match.

A gasp went up as Mikael's foot slipped. He frowned as the bigger man gave him a huge push, and he went flying across the line onto his butt. He stared at the man in disbelief. He couldn't believe he had lost. The Delanor's man had his arms in the air and was walking around and stomping the ground in victory. The crowd booed.

Slowly, Mikael got to his feet and put out his hand. The man shook it and then went back to his display of masculine aggression. Mikael began to walk back to his clan's bench. He was in shock.

Lyzette's eyes were full of tears. What was happening?

The announcer came on and announced the winner and that the exchange of power would begin in five minutes. People rushed around on the field and set up tables. Someone brought in a large box that looked like a safe and placed it on a table. Three men stood guard around it with stun guns out.

Lyzette was trying to understand. Losing wasn't how it was supposed to go. Mikael was the kind of person that made things happen and always won. Maybe she was bringing him bad luck.

"And now," the announcer spoke. "The exchange of power will begin. Will the Markanor please take the field?"

Mikael came out on the field dressed in a black suit with a purple handkerchief tucked in the pocket. His face was carefully schooled not to show any emotion. Lyzette wished she could console him, but she didn't know how. She couldn't offer him the small comfort of taking her body since she was tainted. He didn't want to touch her.

He took the microphone and began his speech.

"As you probably all know, our clan has been in power for the past century. Perhaps it is time for a change. I want you all to know that I am honored to have served as your ruler for a decade, and I hope that Marka will prosper under the new reign."

Mikael unlocked the box and took out a massive ceremonial crown. He placed it on his head, and she could see it was heavy.

"Will the Delanor's interim please step forward to accept the crown?" the announcer said.

A man walked out onto the field. He wore a cloak and walked slowly. He seemed old or injured. He grabbed the microphone from the announcer.

"That won't be necessary. The Delanor is here," he said, throwing back his hood and revealing his face.

It was Deese, and he was back from the dead.

# CHAPTER 18

"What the hell are you doing here?" Mikael said. He was appalled. Deese was the person who had tried to hurt Lyzette. He ran at him, but the security guards stopped him before he could get his hands on the bastard.
"I'm here because you lost," he said, a victorious smile on his face. "And I won."

Mikael struggled while security held him back. The bastard. How could he be here? Mikael thought it would be bad to hand the crown over to Deese's lackey. It would be much worse to give it to Deese himself.

"Let me go," he shouted at the security guards. "Let me go!" He shook his arms violently, and they released him. He took a deep breath and pulled himself together. Then he put his hands on the crown.

"I, the Markanor, do at this moment transfer power to the clan of..."

Deese interrupted him, holding up one hand, palm out.

"I don't want your silly crown," he said.

Mikael was thoroughly puzzled now.

"What do you mean you don't want the crown? You tipped the balance of power. Your clan is in control now. You are the head of your group, so I must transfer the power."

Deese made a dismissive gesture and then looked pained as if it hurt him to move. For the first time, Mikael wondered why Deese wasn't dead. The stun gun must not have delivered a full charge. That was the only thing that would explain it. He had only been stunned. But the amount of electricity he received was difficult for anyone to absorb. It was a wonder Deese could even walk.

"I. Don't. Want. The. Crown." He said. "Pay attention, please. I am taking the forfeit."

A murmur ran through the crowd at this strange and unprecedented announcement.

"What?"

"I want my forfeit."

"All right. Anything I own."

Deese smiled, and Mikael knew there would be trouble. He hadn't finished his revenge, and he wasn't giving up. This man would never stop until he had vengeance.

"I want Lyzette," he said.

Mikael stared at Deese.

"You can't have Lyzette, she's a human."

"She's a slave," Deese corrected. "I believe you registered her at the records office as your property."

Mikael winced. It was true.

"You can't have her."

"I can. I can take anything you own in exchange for the crown, Mikael, and you know it."

"Deese," he said, trying to be reasonable. "You've always wanted to be the Markanor. Think of commanding an entire planet."

The man smiled. Mikael could see he didn't want it anymore. He only wanted to see Mikael suffer. He had figured out Lyzette was the way to do it. She was important to him. He wondered if everyone else could see something that he couldn't.

"The girl. I only want the girl. She's just a slave, Mikael. Get another one. They're a dime a dozen, aren't they? The slave market is full of lovely women."

Mikael faced him, unable to believe that this man was taking Lyzette away from him again. There was nothing he could do to stop him. He was helpless, and it made him crazy. He curled his hands into fists and wished he could punch him in the face. Deese laughed when he saw the movement.

He quickly ran through his options. They were limited. He didn't have any choice. He had to let him take Lyzette and then go after her immediately before he had a chance to hurt her in any way.

"If you don't give me the forfeit, then you're in breach of your crown duties, and the penalty is life in prison or death." He smiled again. "Your choice," he said.

Mikael turned to his box seats, but Lyzette wasn't there. What had happened to her?

She was already walking out on the field, her face expressionless. She was giving herself up.

"Lyzette. No," he said.

"My life is worth nothing compared to yours," she said. "These people need you. Nobody needs me."

She turned to the Delanor, and he saw a muscle jump in her jaw. She was not as calm as she looked.

"I'm ready to go," she said.

"Lyzette." Mikael felt like his heart was being torn out.

"Here, sign this," Deese said, shoving a paper at Mikael. "It confirms I own her now."

Numbly, Mikael signed it. He looked up at Lyzette. She tried to smile at him, but it didn't quite reach her eyes.

"Enough good-byes, you two," Deese said. "She's mine now."

He waved the paper at Mikael.

"And I say we're going."

Deese sauntered off the field, followed by Lyzette.

She didn't look back.

---

Lyzette couldn't believe she was at the mercy of this cruel man again. He got into the carriage, and she followed, sitting across from him.

"Sit here, next to me," he said. "I want a preview of what's to come."

She moved slowly to his side of the carriage. When the horses started unexpectedly, she fell into him. He put his hands out. He did not intend to catch her. Instead, he placed both palms on her breasts and squeezed, copping a feel.

She sat down beside him in disgust when he let her go. Immediately, he slid a hand into the slit of her long blue dress, moving it slowly up her leg until he brushed her panties. She had to clench her teeth together to bear it. He was her master now.

She realized that she had been very wrong about Mikael. He never treated her like a slave, not since the beginning of their relationship. He had always concerned himself with what she wanted. She had never been a slave to Mikael.

But she was a slave now, there was no doubt about it.

"Put this on," he said, handing her a necklace. She obediently fastened it around her neck.

"Touch me," he told her next, unzipping his pants. Very reluctantly, she freed his erect cock that was quite long but not very thick. She wrapped her hand around it and pumped up and down.

"Yeah, so good," he said, closing his eyes. A minute later, he came all over the carriage floor.

"The other slaves will clean it up, don't worry," he said. He tucked himself back in his pants. "You don't have to do anything like that. Just service me whenever I want you to, for the rest of your life. It may be short if I decide to kill you," he added as an afterthought.

Lyzette said nothing. She tried to wipe her hand off on her dress discretely.

Deese closed his eyes and appeared to be resting. That's when Lyzette wondered how the hell he was alive when she had seen his dead body lying on the floor. Mikael set the stun gun to lethal when he shot Deese. Had it malfunctioned?

She didn't worry about it too long. She was his slave now. She needed to figure out a way to cope with being around Deese for the rest of her life.

She had no idea what to do. There wasn't a team of women to help her this time. She stared out the window.

The carriage was going straight across the plains to the mountains. Before, when she had been his captive, they blindfolded her and took her to his townhouse in the city.

It appeared they were heading to his mansion, way out of town. She turned around, trying to see which way they had come. If she managed to escape, she would need to remember which way to go to get back. She had seen it on a survival TV show. You always looked behind you to know what to look for when you returned.

Twenty minutes later, they pulled into a huge manor house. Deese passed her into a servant's care.

"Make her ready for me. I will have supper and a bath, and then I will return to my chambers. I'll see you later," he said to Lyzette. She couldn't suppress a shudder.

She knew there would be no rescue this time. Mikael had signed the papers. Legally, she was Deese's, and he could do whatever he wanted with her.

The servant took her to the bathhouse and stripped her down, making her get in the hot water. An old woman scrubbed her down until her skin hurt. At least she was clean. She let Lyzette out and handed her a towel. The servant led her to her room and pointed to a chair.

"Your night clothes are there. Stay here until he calls you," she said, giving Lyzette a look of disgust. Then she went out and locked the door. Lyzette sighed and looked at what was on the chair. A leather bra with holes for her breasts to stick out and leather crotchless panties. Great. She didn't put them on, but went to the bed and got in, discarding the towel on the nightstand. She closed her eyes and slipped her hand down between her legs. She had been doing it every day since Mikael stopped making love to her. Her other hand plumped her breast as her finger slid up and down her slit. She thought of Mikael and how he had touched her. His kiss. His body covering hers. How he filled her up.

She came quickly, her body shuddering. But it wasn't like with Mikael. It scratched her itch but didn't get rid of it. Only he could give her satisfaction.

Maybe it was good things ended this way. She wouldn't be able to take it if Mikael sent her away because she was tainted.

She would be used goods now, for sure. But it didn't matter. She would never see Mikael again.

Her eyes closed and she slept.

---

She woke to the feel of someone snuffling her neck and groping hands all over her body where she didn't want them. What the hell? She put her hands on him and pushed hard. He went flying off the bed and landed with a thump.

"You fucking bitch," she heard Deese say from the floor.

She was up in a second and across the room, trying to cover herself.

"You're mine. You have to do what I say. And if you don't," he said, getting up slowly and going over to the table and picking up something long and black. "If you don't, I will enjoy teaching you a lesson."

A whip. It was a real whip.

"I don't tolerate insubordination from my slaves," he said.

Lyzette froze in place. He was going to whip her. And it was going to hurt. Then her self-protective instincts kicked in.

"You don't want to do that," she said, trying to sound coy. "If I'm bleeding and crying, how will I suck your cock?"

"You could do both," he said, and she saw that he was getting hard, and he let the whip drop back on the table.

"Not very well. I need to focus on you and your needs," she said. "Because I belong to you now. Thank goodness, now I have a real man to serve."

Lyzette thought that she was laying it on a bit too thick, but Deese seemed to like it.

"That's right. Come here," he said.

She sauntered over, trying not to tremble because of her intense fear.

He pulled her to him and kissed her. It was disgusting, but she knew better than to show her real emotions. All she had to remember was that kissing him was better than being flogged. Wasn't it?

His hands began roaming again. He put both hands on her breasts and massaged them, tweaking her nipples until they were tight and round.

He took this as a sign of her arousal and dropped his hand between her legs where she was still dripping and slippery from her self-stimulation and dreams of Mikael.

"So wet for me," he said when he felt her.

"How about I suck you first," she said, trying to look seductive. She wanted to avoid having him fuck her for as long as possible.

He swallowed, looking at her red lips.

"Just think of your big cock going in and out of these lips," she whispered. She had no idea where she was getting her acting skills. Her desperation fueled creativity.

"Yes," he said, breathing heavily. "Yes."

He sat down on the bed and dragged her roughly down to her knees on the floor.

"Suck me, bitch," he said. "You're mine now. And you do what I command, slave."

She didn't remind him that it had been her idea to blow him. It was better if he thought he was in control.

And that's when Lyzette had an epiphany. If he only thought he was in control, that meant that he wasn't. And if he wasn't. Then she, Lyzette, was in control of her life for the first time.

She was amazed at her brilliant conclusion.

"Suck me," he said, and grabbed her hair, pushing her mouth down to his erection.

She would suck him, and it would be disgusting, but she would do it because it was a part of her plan.

Lyzette had a plan.

She was in control. And that, she found, made all the difference.

# CHAPTER 19

Lyzette sucked off Deese, and he had wanted to cum on her breasts, so of course he had. Then he lay back on the bed. Perhaps he was tired. The stun gun must have hurt him, even if it hadn't killed him. He seemed like an old man. She snuck away as soon as he fell asleep and showered off his cum.

Now she sat at a table beside the whip and worked out the details of her plan. She would prevent him from fucking her as long as she could. She would fill a bag with all the food she could get tomorrow. She would walk off into the mountains, and she wouldn't come back.

It was dark outside, and she could see the moons out the window. Deese snored on the bed. For the first time in her life, Lyzette felt like she was going to make things happen. She was in charge. It was a heady feeling she had never experienced before.

She knew then her mother had been wrong, probably about a lot of things, but definitely about taking action. Her mother always told her that she had to accept whatever happened to her and make the best of it.

But now Lyzette knew that wasn't true. She felt a strength inside of her that had been there all along, waiting to rise. It had got her through a lot of terrible things in her life, and it would help her now as well.

The next day, she put her plan into place. She was terrified. When she woke up in the early morning light, she saw that Deese had left. The maid that brought her breakfast informed Lyzette he always swam for two hours in the morning in a nearby lake.

Perfect. She had an hour.

She ducked into the kitchen and asked the cook for some food for her hike. She explained how she liked to go on long walks. The cook gave her a dirty look but filled the bag with all sorts of snacks that were perfect for a long trip. After she hid, she would make the journey back to the city. It would take a long time, but she could do it.

Her well-spring of confidence was new and amazing. Lyzette couldn't believe how good it felt to believe in herself. She had never thought she could do anything before. After her epiphany, she knew she could never go back to being her old, unhappy self.

She would free herself from this madness. She would get off this damned planet. And she would make a new life for herself the way that she wanted it. She told another maid that she was going for her daily hike and got a vicious stare for her efforts, but she didn't care. She was starting a new life today.

She headed up a trail that led to the peaks. She got off the trail as soon as she could and made her own way. She splashed through some streams, hoping the water would make it hard for dogs to track her.

The day was beautiful, and she enjoyed herself. She made her way further and further up the mountain until she came to a bit of a plain between the peaks. It seemed like a good place to stop and rest. There was a lovely little stream that looked clean. Lyzette took a drink and ate a few pieces of dried meat and fruit. It was the most delicious meal she could remember. She felt free and happy in the mountains and wished she could stay forever.

She kept walking as long as she could. When the sun went down, she rolled up in a blanket and went straight to sleep. She was exhausted.

Lyzette woke to the sound of aircraft landing beside her in the middle of the night. She sat up and put her hand up to block the lights. What was a personal aircraft doing out here in the mountains?

But she didn't wonder long. Two big men got out and came towards her. The Delanor's men. They pulled her to her feet and dragged her back to the aircraft, throwing her inside so hard she banged her head. Tears filled her eyes.

She felt let down that her escape attempt didn't work. Then she realized that she had tasted freedom for a few hours. If she had done it once, she could do it again.

Lyzette wished she could share her new self with someone who would care. Of course, Mikael's face popped into her head, and she felt a longing for him. But she pushed the image and the feeling away, focusing on what she could do. She could affect her reality. She could change things. She could do this.

189

Her mother was wrong. Her mother would have said, spread your legs and keep him happy, so he doesn't use that whip on you. But Lyzette had made a decision based on what she wanted. Maybe she was about to pay for her choices, she thought. The personal aircraft landed in the courtyard of the Delanor's mansion. But it had been worth it to discover her inner strength. She would get away from the insanity and create a life for herself.

No one was going to stop her.

---

Fifteen minutes later, Lyzette still believed that she was going to get away. When the lash of the whip bit into her back, she was less certain her escape attempt had been a good idea.

The Delanor was furious.

She couldn't help the screams. She had no idea it was painful to be whipped. If she had, she wouldn't have been caught.

"What were you thinking, you little bitch?" he cried.

Lyzette didn't tell him what she had thought as the blood ran down her back and dripped onto the floor. She was leaning over the table in his room, completely naked as he flogged her.

"Did you honestly think I wouldn't find you and that I would trust my slaves? I have a tracking device on you!"

He hit her again, and she screamed. It fucking hurt, she couldn't help it, though she was sure he liked to hear her pain.

A tracking device? The necklace he had given her when she arrived. Why had she continued wearing it?

He lifted his arm again, and Lyzette cringed. She waited for more agony, but it didn't come. The Delanor gasped for breath and couldn't bring his arm back far enough to swing. Lyzette wondered how close he had come to death. He seemed terribly weak.

Maybe she could kill him.

The thought popped into her head, and once it appeared, she couldn't get it out of her mind. If she killed Deese, it would solve a lot of problems.

"I'm going to give you the beating of your life," he said, but his voice sounded feeble. He fell into the chair. He didn't seem like he could catch his breath. Lyzette lifted her head. "I just have to rest a second. Moorlal!" A man entered from the hallway.

"Yes, sir," the man said. Lyzette looked at him, and he met her eyes with compassion for a moment before he quickly looked away.

"Give this slave ten more lashes," he ordered in a quiet tone, still gasping for breath.

The man looked her up and down dispassionately.

"Respectfully, sir, she can't take ten more lashes. You'll kill her. The blood loss alone will weaken her, and she doesn't have the strength to stand it."

Lyzette disagreed. She could take it. Still, she didn't want to have to endure ten more lashes. She would inevitably pass out if she didn't die from blood loss or sheer mental agony. Didn't they beat people to death on Earth a long time ago? Maybe the man was trying to help her, and she sent a silent thank you his way if he was.

"Good," Deese said. "I want her dead."

"I thought you wanted your revenge for Mikael fucking your girl and ruining your life. You can't use her for revenge if she's dead," he said, reasonably. "Your plan is on track. And you need her alive to make it work. Just because you're angry, sir, is not a good reason to throw away years of planning."

"You're probably right," Deese mumbled. Lyzette thought he was drifting into unconsciousness. A moment later, the servant caught him and threw him over his shoulder.

"He'll be out all night, now," he told her. "I'm one of Mikael's men. I infiltrated Deese's clan last year. Whatever you do, don't tell anyone about me. And you ought to thank your lucky stars he's sick right now. You could be dead or so broken that you wouldn't even recognize yourself."

Lyzette swallowed hard. She knew that now.

"I can't tell you much, but I'll let you know this. You're bait for Mikael. This disgusting situation is all about Deese getting revenge. He wanted to rape you in front of him but when that didn't work, he upped the ante. He still wants to do that, but he's going all-in. You're both in big trouble, girl. I admire you for trying to get away, but there's worse coming, you should know."

"Like what?" Lyzette said.

"I'll be the one beaten to death if I tell you," he said, shaking his head. "There's no way to disarm it. Rip it out, throw it, and get the hell away as fast as you can."

"What? I don't understand."

"You will," he said, grimly. "Oh, and one more thing. He's too weak to fuck you right now. I don't know when that will change. I have to go now. Good luck."

* * *

Lyzette didn't understand anything until she walked down a long hallway into an arena. The stage looked like a ring where animals fought. The room was dark and had a strange smell. A bright spotlight illuminated the ring.

Her captors laid her down on a table with her wrists tied together and stretched over her head. She had on the leather outfit from her first night with Deese. The servants put her feet on the table far apart. Her breasts pushed up out of the holes in the bra. Her sex was on display in the crotchless underwear.

She was scared and humiliated, but she tried to stay calm. Somehow she would find a way to escape. She was going to get away from Deese without being broken. She felt confident. But when the people started filing in — all men — and began hooting and hollering things at her, she wasn't sure anymore.

Her hopes collapsed when they brought in Mikael with his hands tied behind his back. He walked stiffly and looked exhausted. His old bruises were almost faded, but new ones took their place. She wondered how he got them. Had he been fighting to get to her?

He gave her one anguished look before his guards dragged him to the side. He sat down in a chair where he would have a perfect view of Deese fucking her.

When Deese came out, things got worse.

He looked invigorated. Lyzette was instantly afraid. If he had recovered, he would be back to his old strength and could perform once again. The one thing she had been counting on to save her had vanished.

"As many of you know," he said into the microphone, "Mikael and I have been enemies for many years. You also know he was cruel enough to lure my girlfriend away from me and fuck her. The time has come for me to return the favor."

He turned and smiled at Mikael.

"I'm going to do the same to him. His new consort is a favorite of his, and he's going to watch me take her, just like all of you," he said. A roar went up from the crowd, and Lyzette swallowed hard.

Deese walked over, and the crowd gave a cheer. He came to stand beside her and played with her tits while he whispered in her ear.

"You will act like I'm fucking you, or I will pull out a gun and shoot Mikael point blank. Work hard, sweetie, or he dies," he said. "It doesn't matter if I fuck you or not. Either way he's tortured."

She stared at him as he moved around to stand between her legs and undid his pants. She was stunned. He couldn't get it up.

He made a thrust with his hips, and she screamed, a second too late. Had anyone noticed? He gave her a menacing look, and she writhed as he pressed his hips against her, trying to moan as if she was being raped. She could feel his flaccid cock touching her sex. Gross.

Then he found a rhythm, and she imagined that he was raping her. She remembered her fear and her the moans of terror became realistic. She made horrible sounds with each thrust of his hips.

She screamed several times, for variety. She was worried about being convincing enough. Would he pull out a gun and kill Mikael in front of her?

Lyzette twisted her head a little and looked at Mikael. She could see him. He was hurting. He had a look of horror on his face.

She felt terrible, but she couldn't help it. There was no way that Lyzette was going to risk his life to spare him mental anguish. She couldn't have him, but she would do anything to save him.

That's when it hit her. She would do anything to save his life because she loved him.

Now she could never have him, but she would save him just the same.

# CHAPTER 20

Mikael couldn't believe the scene in front of his eyes. He felt like he was going to cry in front of all these people. He hadn't cried since he was a boy.

After everything he had done to get to Lyzette, he had failed her again. It didn't matter that he had people searching the city and that he had tried to get into Deese's compound on three separate occasions. The last time, he had been beaten up so badly he could hardly walk.

Deese was raping her in front of his very eyes. His Lyzette. His funny little Lyzette, who couldn't stop saying strange quotes from her mother and radiated fragility. He remembered her initial reluctance to be with him and her unbelievable response when he had made love to her.

He swallowed and blinked back tears. He needed to pull himself together. He couldn't show weakness in front of this crowd.

It seemed to go on forever, and Mikael thought he would vomit when she started crying. Finally, Deese groaned and pushed against her. He shoved himself back in his pants and raised his arms overhead, victorious. He came to Mikael so he could laugh in his face.

The crowd started chanting his name. Lyzette curled up on the table and wept. Mikael thought it was over. Now they would take him back to his cell, and he could let the tears fall.

But it wasn't over yet.

Deese was signaling for someone else to come out. There was more coming in this freak show. He wondered what the Delanor had come up with now.

It was a doctor in a white coat.

Mikael knew Deese had a cruel streak, and he hoped Deese wasn't going to do something horrible to Lyzette. She had been hurt enough already. He hoped nothing repulsive was about to occur.

The doctor forced Lyzette to sit up. He took out some instruments and laid them on a white cloth. In the meantime, Deese picked up the microphone again.

"I've got some more entertainment for you today. Do you want more?" he said, working the crowd. They screamed, and it hurt Mikael's ears. They were already ringing from his earlier pummeling.

"My friend here is going to help us out. He's going to make Lyzette a scorching hot girlfriend."

He laughed to himself. No one else laughed because they didn't know what he meant.

"What you see in the doctor's hands is a tiny explosive."

The crowd went crazy.

"Yes. Scientists on Earth developed it. Earth is the home planet of our little slut of a slave. Isn't that right, Lyzette?"

She didn't even look up. She stared listlessly down at her lap.

"It can be inserted anywhere in the body. I nearly put it where the sun doesn't shine, as they say. But I didn't want to give Mikael any pleasure before he died. So I've decided to embed it in her lip. Doctor?"

The doctor loaded the device into a gun. Lyzette thought it looked like something used to get her ears pierced.

He pulled her lip out and placed the gun against her skin. With a deft flick of his finger, he pulled the trigger and shot the explosive into her. It looked like a lip stud and poked up slightly above her lower lip.

She made no noise. She didn't acknowledge the doctor's presence. Mikael felt devastated to see her that way. He remembered how she had looked the day he noticed her artwork was fantastic. When she realized that he meant what he was saying about her creations, her eyes lit up with happiness.

The contrast with the way she looked now was too brutal for him to contemplate, and he turned his eyes away.

"Thank you, doctor. Can you arm it, please?"

The doctor pressed on the device, and it began blinking.

"Perfect. That will do, doctor. That will do."

He strode into the center of the ring and held out his arms. The crowd roared again.

"Now, the next thing to do is to tell you something I've learned about these two. They're lovebirds!"

Mikael froze. Lyzette lifted her head and looked him straight in the eyes with an expression of surprise on her face.

"Yes, Mikael. You talk in your sleep, you know. And the night you spent in my cell proved to be quite informative. Can you believe it? The Markanor of the entire planet has fallen in love with a slave."

The crowd booed.

"I know. I know. It's inappropriate, and I think we should severely punish them both. Do you think they should be punished?"

The crowd started cheering again.

"And what better way to punish lovers than to take one of the most pleasurable things two people in love can experience, and turn it into something that will kill them both."

The men started chanting.

"Kill them. Kill them. Kill them."

"Mikael, if you would come over here."

His guard gave him a poke with a gun and Mikael got to his feet. He tried not to show his pain. He couldn't help being stiff from all the bruises on his torso and broken ribs.

"Stand up, slave."

She gave Deese a look of hatred, then slowly got to her feet. Mikael wanted to cover her up from all the prying eyes, but that was the least of his problems right now. How was he going to stop this?

"And now. Our two lovebirds will treat us all to one last show of their affection. A kiss."

"Kiss, kiss, kiss, kiss!" The crowd wound up to a fever pitch.

"Don't worry about your safety. These wonderful little explosives can be set precisely so the explosion won't leave this ring."

The chanting stopped as the men realized Deese was going to do something dangerous. Mikael noticed some of the smarter ones leaving immediately, but that left all of his dumbest clan members. One of them yelled, "Explode that whore," making Mikael even more nauseated. What kind of men were they to be saying such things?

"Yes, yes," Deese said soothingly. "All in good time. First, the rules of the game."

Mikael stood in front of Lyzette. He had his hands tied behind his back, and she had hers tied in front.

They were about a foot apart, and he could see a tiny bump on her lip where the bomb was. The other end of the explosive protruded from the skin under her lip. It had a knob holding it in place.

"You cannot touch, other than your lips."

He walked around them, his hands clasped behind his back.

"Don't try anything fishy, Mikael. Lyzette, we all know that you're not intelligent enough to come up with anything innovative."

Lyzette met his eyes while Deese turned and faced the crowd.

"Kiss her until the explosive detonates. Don't worry, it's a hair trigger. It won't take much pressure."

"I love you," he whispered, looking deep into her eyes. He had to tell her, and this might be his last chance. Her eyes grew round, but she didn't say it back.

"Be ready," Lyzette said instead.

Mikael held his breath.

"If you refuse to kiss her," Deese went on, "she will be shot dead in front of you. We will torture you until you wish you had died while kissing your love."

A man stepped forward with a big weapon and aimed it at Lyzette. Mikael showed no reaction, but his brain was working. He wondered what Lyzette meant.

"Are you ready?" The crowd hooted. He opened a door that let him out of the ring and into the stands. He still held the microphone.

"Mikael and Lyzette. You may kiss for the last time," he said.

The cheers became deafening, and Mikael started to move toward her, knowing that any hesitation could spell her immediate death. Once they were clearly going to kiss, Deese motioned for the man with the gun to lower it so everyone could see.

Lyzette kept her eyes on him as he slowly moved towards her. She stretched up as if she were reaching to press her lips to his.

"Kiss, kiss, kiss," the crowd roared.

He shifted his weight from side to side, trying to be ready for whatever was about to happen. With his eyes on hers, he could see the precise moment that she decided to take action.

Her hands came up like lightning. She grabbed the knob on the end of the bomb. He saw her fingers turning white from the pressure. Lyzette pulled viciously.

The device ripped out of her lip. There was blood everywhere, but she threw it away. They started running.

The crowd turned insane, screaming righteous fury. Lyzette deprived them of an execution.

A moment later, when the bomb hit the ground, there was an explosion that launched them into the hallway. The force hurled Lyzette into the wall, and Mikael ended up on the floor. They immediately got up and started running aaway. They stumbled but went as fast as they could.

Chaos reigned behind them as the crowd began to riot. They heard Deese howling in a rage since the microphone was still on. The howls could be roars of pain. Lyzette had thrown the bomb in Deese's direction.

When they got to the street, they met police coming in. Lyzette collapsed, and a burly officer picked her up and took her to a waiting ambulance. Mikael made it there under his power, but when he reached the ambulance, the stress of recent events took its toll and he collapsed.

"You'll find the Delanor in there. Talk to Moorlal. He should have a video of everything that happened. It should certainly be enough to arrest him."

The police officer nodded, and a squad of men followed him into the building.

The paramedics already had Lyzette's wound staunched, and she lay on a stretcher. They cut off her leather outfit and put a hospital gown on her.

"Let's go," Mikael said. When the paramedics looked more carefully and saw their ruler, they moved even faster. A moment later, he felt his vision blurring.

"No disrespect, sir, but I think we'd better get you both to the hospital immediately and have you checked over. You're both going into shock, and I believe you have some broken ribs."

# CHAPTER 21

Lyzette's eyes fluttered open. She closed them again almost immediately. She didn't want to be awake. It was nicer being unconscious. There was no noise, no pain, and no humiliation.

"Lyzette, sweetie? Are you awake?"

It was Mikael's voice. He was alive.

She opened her eyes to confirm what she had heard. He stood beside her as she lay on the hospital bed.

"Lyzzie?" he said, leaning forward and taking her hand as she gazed at him sorrowfully. "What's wrong? Do you need pain medication? Should I call the doctor? What can I do?" He paused and thought about his next words. "The doctor said there were no signs that Deese did anything to you." He seemed worried. She put out a hand and shook her head.

"He didn't?"

She shook her head again.

"Are you sure you're all right?"

She wasn't sure if she was all right or not, but she knew he didn't need to call the doctor. No doctor could help treat the pain she felt.

She turned her head, looking away from Mikael as she felt tears come to her eyes. She had almost buried her emotions while she was Deese's prisoner. She couldn't ignore them when he was sitting beside her.

She loved him, but she was Deese's slave by law, and she could never have Mikael. Even if she hadn't been the Delanor's slave, she would have been Mikael's slave, and he could no more marry a slave than he could cut out his heart. She felt like doing something to her heart; that way, it wouldn't hurt so much to love him.

She turned away and curled up in a ball, pulling the covers tightly around her. The blanket brushed the bandages on her lip. It hurt, but she didn't care. Maybe she could go back to sleep. She wanted to escape. She was tired of everything.

"Lyzette?" Mikael asked. He had to do something, just like a man; he could not wait. He came around to the other side of the bed and sat down on a chair, where she lay with her eyes tightly closed. "Please, Lyz. What's wrong? I want to help."

She flashed back to the night when they'd been waiting to kiss each other. He said he loved her. Didn't he? It felt like a dream. How could she explain what she was feeling? Lyzette swallowed to keep from bursting into tears.

He leaned forward and kissed her on the forehead. When she lifted her reluctant eyelids to look at him, she could see that his eyes seemed bright. She found her voice somewhere deep inside her and dragged it out. She did it for him.

"It doesn't matter, Mikael."

"It does," he interrupted.

"No. The problems of a slave don't matter," she said. "I know you think I'm more than a slave, but I'm not."

From the expression on his face, he didn't like what she was saying.

"We can never be together. I am Deese's property now, and he can do whatever he likes with me. I doubt he's going to give me back to you. Whatever this is," she waved her hand weakly back and forth between them. "Our feelings are irrelevant. Circumstances doomed our relationship from the beginning."

He stared at her.

"Of course. You don't know."

"Know what, Mikael?" she asked, feeling discouraged. She didn't know and didn't care.

He took her hand. "You're not a slave anymore, Lyzette."

She turned her head to look at him sharply.

"What? What are you playing at, Mikael? Don't toy with my mind," she said, frowning. "You told me that the only way a slave could become free is if the slave died or left the planet. Unfortunately, I haven't died, nor have I left the world."

"No," he said, with a happy light in his eye.

She gazed at him. What did he mean?

"You're alive and still on Marka, that's true, thank goodness. But I told you one more way that a slave can get her freedom."

"Well, you did say if the slave's master died, they were granted freedom. But you're alive and well in front of me."

"I'm not your master anymore, Lyzette."

"Oh, of course," she said, still feeling a bit woozy. She looked up at Mikael, unwilling to say it.

"Deese is dead, Lyzette."

"Dead?" she said, skeptically. "We thought that before."

"Well, I inspected the body and watched as it burned. I'm certain this time. He's gone for good. His successor is a reasonable man, who will change his clan for the better, I hope."

Lyzette sat up. Her mind reeled at the sudden change in her circumstances. Her lip was pulsing, and she put her hand up to touch the bandage.

"You mean I could get up and walk out of here, and no one would be able to stop me?"

"You could," he said, smiling.

"And I could get on a shuttle and go anywhere in the galaxy and start my life over?" Her eyes lit up at the thought that she could do what she had dreamed about after her revelation at Deese's house. She stared off into space and imagined getting on a shuttle and flying off into the unknown.

"You could," he said again, a little sadly this time.

"And even you, the Markanor of the whole planet couldn't tell me what I should do. Only me. I would get to decide," she said, feeling a power flowing through her, strong as a river.

"That's right," he said. He looked deflated, but Lyzette was so caught up in her delight at the thought of freedom that she didn't notice.

He leaned forward, putting his elbows on his knees and dropping his head into his hands. When he looked depressed, Lyzette finally clued in that something was wrong.

"Mikael?" she asked, studying him. He didn't move. She saw something drop onto the floor, and when she leaned over to see what it was, she was shocked to see it looked like water.

She hopped off the bed and knelt beside his chair.

"Leave me alone, Lyzette," he said, and his voice sounded small. "I'm a fucking idiot, okay? Just leave me alone."

His breathing was shaky. She needed to know, so she reached up and pulled his hands away. He turned his face away from hers and wrenched one hand out of her grip to swipe at his eyes.

"Look, just leave me alone, okay? I made a mistake. I see that now. But you don't have to rub my nose in it. I'll buy you a ticket to any place you want, Lyzette, and you can go and make all your dreams come true."

She didn't say anything, but moved closer to him and held his big hand in her small ones. "Look at me."

He wouldn't.

"Look at me, please?" she said.

He turned, and there was a small tear running down his cheek. She reached up and gently rubbed it away with her thumb.

"I'm sorry."

"It's okay, Lyzette. You can't choose who you love."

"No," she said forcefully. "Listen. I'm sorry that I didn't tell you sooner. I didn't mean to cause you pain, Mikael." She looked away, pressed her lips together and then met his eyes again. "I love you. I love you so much," she said, her voice catching in her throat and her eyes shining with tears. "But I didn't want to let myself. It was too hard to think about our future."

Mikael nodded, and she could tell he felt guilty for her horrible circumstances.

"Those things weren't your fault, Mik. Look at me."

He looked up.

"They weren't your fault. And I see now that they needed to happen."

"Needed to? What do you mean?"

"When I was Deese's prisoner, I realized something. I can control things in my life. I can make things happen. And I can change my actions and the outcomes I get will change, too."

He looked at her in amazement.

"You found your inner strength."

"Exactly. I always thought that things just happened to me. But now I see I can do the same things, or different things and events will be affected."

"Wow," Mikael looked floored. "I see it in your eyes. It's in your whole demeanor. You found your power, Lyzette."

"Yeah," she said, agreeing enthusiastically. "That's what gave me the courage to do what I did last night. Your spy told me that I could rip it out. I never thought I could do it. I thought if I let you kiss me, you would die. Even though it wouldn't matter too much if I died, I couldn't let that happen to you because I love you."

"Do you mean it, Lyzette?"

"I mean it," she said. "With all my heart."

"Well, then," he said. "Come here." He patted his lap. "Flip over your forearm."

Lyzette flipped it over to show the three interlocking circles.

"You know this isn't only a brand, right? Everyone in my clan has one of these."

"I didn't know that. I thought you only put them on your slaves."

"Nope. The slaves have red circles."

He pulled out a blue tube.

"What's that?"

"It's permanent skin dye, Lyzette. Do you know the color of the Markanor's family circles?" She shook her head as he flipped his forearm over. "Purple." He opened the tube of paint.

"But Mikael," Lyzette said. "I'm not a member of your family."

He stopped and recapped the tube of paint and set it out on the bed.

"That's true. Not yet. Lyzette," he said, taking her hand and tracing his finger around the circles on her arm.

"Yes?"

He took a deep breath and looked deeply into her eyes.

"I love you. Will you marry me?"

She drew in a quick breath. She was surprised. She hadn't expected it. Lyzette stared at him with her mouth open.

"Lyzzie, love? Could you answer? Please?" he said, looking desperately afraid.

"I will," she said, wrapping her arms around him and wishing she could kiss him properly. He kissed her all over her face — everywhere except her lips.

"Lyzzie, I love you so much," he said. "I want to marry you as soon as possible. I want you to be my wife. You can go anywhere and do anything your heart desires as long as you come back to me."

Lyzette sniffed.

"You own me, Lyz, heart and soul. I need you more than anything. I am your slave."

"I need you too, Mikael. My mother used to have this pillow with a saying on it."

"Lyzette, I don't even know your mom, and I don't like her. I don't want to hear what your mother has to say."

"No," she laughed. "Listen. It's appropriate. It wasn't something she said. Someone gave it to her. I don't think she ever believed it. The pillow said: If you love something, let it go. If it comes back to you, it's yours. If it doesn't, it never was."

"Then I let you go, Lyzette. You're free."

"And I choose to stay here," she said, holding him close. "Right in your arms."

# CHAPTER 22

The woman walked through the crowded gallery, barely glancing at the works of art. She was beautiful and had a self-confidence that was obvious to anyone looking at her. This woman clearly knew who she was and her place in the universe.

She wore a black pencil skirt that went to her knees, paired with black high heels. Her long-sleeved shirt was black and stretched over her top, conforming to her body and demurely covering her large breasts. She styled her long dark brown hair in an elegant bun at the nape of her neck.

She conveyed an aura of distinction and more than one woman in the room wished that she had been born so lucky.

In the main room of the gallery, the ruler of Marka started his speech. He was promoting the high-profile artist. The woman's heels clicked more quickly as she increased her pace, knowing she was late. She made her way as unobtrusively as possible to the front of the crowd.

She listened to the speech, smiling a little at some parts. And when he met her eye, her heart sped up a little.

"And now, I would like to open the new art show, Inner Strength. Please help me welcome Lyzette Pauvre, the Markana!"

The crowd applauded politely, and the servers began to circulate again with flutes of champagne and Markan delicacies.

Lyzette moved forward to where Mikael was speaking with a diplomat. Before she reached him, she was accosted by a blonde woman. It was Raimey, and Lyzette barely recognized her. She looked completely different.

"Lyzzie," she squealed. "These paintings are excellent. I'm impressed!"

"Thanks, Raimey," Lyzette said, smiling happily to see her old friend.

A man came up behind Raimey and put his hand on her back.

"This is Gordie," she said. "Gord, this is Lyzette. We were slaves together when she first came to Marka. She's the Markana now."

"Nice to meet you, Markana," he said, extending his forearm. Lyzette tapped hers on top of his.

"Nice to meet you too. I'm sorry I can't chat longer, Raimey, but I have to mingle."

Lyzette was delighted to see Raimey again, and would be sure to reconnect in the future. She missed Raimey. She had been such a help to her when Lyzette had first arrived here, lost and confused.

She said good-bye and continued her way to Mikael.

"Excuse me, Markana?" a man said, stopping her again before she could get to Mikael.

"Yes?" she said, politely. There were constant interruptions tonight.

"I wanted to thank you for your work on behalf of the slaves. When the legislature passed the edict freeing all the slaves on Marka and giving them citizenship, I couldn't believe it." He choked up and had to look away for a moment. "It meant the world to my daughter. She was a slave for twenty years to a terrible master. We are forever indebted to you for helping us."

"I'm so glad to have been of service, sir. I was a slave myself, so I understand the terrible feelings of powerlessness. Once I had my freedom, I couldn't leave all those other women trapped. Please give your daughter my best."

"I will be sure to do that. Thank you, Markana," he said, kneeling and placing his hand, palm out, on his forehead in a gesture of respect.

She smiled and made a beeline to the refreshment tables where Mikael was loading up a plate. She picked up some food herself and joined him at the table. She was starving.

"Tsk, tsk," he said, keeping his eyes on his plate. "The Markana was late for her gallery opening."

"Mikael," she said in a wheedling tone. "The kids asked for one more story. You know how Margo is. She won't be put off. Jeannette had a cold, so she was clingy. I was ready to go on time. How was I to know that the horse had thrown a shoe? It took Jol fifteen minutes to hitch up another horse and for us to get going. We came as fast as we could."

She stopped when he grinned at her. She sighed.

"You're annoying."

"Sorry, love. Too easy. You were right on time, not late, remember? Maybe you even heard some of the speech I lovingly prepared?"

"I heard it all, for the fiftieth time. But it sounded good this time," she added. She wanted him to know she appreciated the time and effort he put into preparing the speech. "Thanks so much for doing this, Mik. You know I enjoy it."

"I know, I know," he said. "Want to find somewhere to sit down?"

They made their way to a room with a sofa. It faced a large painting of a woman and a man kissing with the world around them exploding.

"Hm," Mikael said, popping a piece of meat into his mouth and staring at the artwork. "This painting is entitled The Kiss of Death. Is this piece just fantasy, Markana? Or does it represent an actual event?"

Lyzette shook her head, laughing a little. As if Mikael hadn't seen all her pieces a million times. He had heard her go on and on about their progress while she was painting them. He even helped her choose the ones for the show.

He knew damn well this painting was her way of trying to get the trauma of the bomb out of her system. It also represented the strength of her love for Mikael. She sometimes felt like she loved him so much, she might explode. And, though she hadn't told anyone this, it was also a representation of their explosive chemistry. Even now, after five years and two kids, she still couldn't get enough of him.

"Mikael," she said. "The official opening is over, and we can probably sneak out of here in the next hour. Will you be ready to go?"

"For sure, sweets. You know black tie isn't my thing. Besides, someone's got her hair in a bun."

Lyzette blushed and put a piece of cheese in her mouth, chewing self-consciously. Mikael had a fantasy he liked to act out where she pretended to be a teacher, and he was a student who had been bad. When she had a bun in her hair, it always made him hot for her. She was thinking about when she got dressed tonight. It had been over a week since they made love, and she needed him.

"Yes, someone does," she said.

"And someone knows what that does to me. Someone is finishing up her food, and we're getting out of here."

Lyzette winked at him and picked up her pickle. Innocently, she slid it into her mouth and then bit it off crisply.

"Be careful, Lyzzie. Don't tease me," he said under his breath. "Or you'll be sorry later."

"Will I?" she whispered. "I hope so."

She saw his chest rising and falling rapidly.

"I'm going to say my goodbyes and head out. Meet me in the front lobby."

"Yes, sir," she said.

"Save it for later, Lyz." He grabbed an olive off her plate and tossed it in his mouth. "And make sure you're not late."

---

Lyzette was on time and soon they headed out of the city. The two full moons shone down, making everything as light as day.

Mikael wrapped his arms around Lyzette, and she laid her head on his chest. They were quiet together, enjoying the night.

"Mikael?" she asked, not moving from her comfortable position.

"Yeah, babe?" he said, looking down at her.

"I can't believe I just opened my fifth show. Do you remember how I was when I first came here?"

"I do, sweetie," he said, softly.

"I thought I had to hide my art or people would laugh at it. Now they pay me thousands of credits to have the privilege of looking at it. It's crazy. It's amazing."

"It is amazing," he said. "And so are you."

He put his hand under her chin and tilted her face up to look at him. She smiled a little, and he kissed her gently. Soon the kiss warmed up, and it got hot. Lyzette knew they had to stop, or she might embarrass herself in the carriage, forcing Jol to pretend like he didn't hear anything.

She pulled away, and Mikael dragged her back.

"Mikael," she whispered, breathless. "Mik. Stop. We have to wait."

"I can't hold on, Lyz," he said, his eyes pleading.

They were still far from home.

"Oh, come on, Mikael. We're a little old for that, aren't we?" Her heart was beating faster.

He smiled, knowing he had her. Then he tapped Jol on the shoulder.

"Hey, Jol, we need to stop at the waterfall."

"Yes, sir," the older man said.

"There's a bonus in it for being patient," Mikael told him, grabbing two blankets from under the seat.

Jol glanced at Lyzette. She gave him an apologetic look, but he waved a hand at her.

They rushed to the waterfall, stumbling and tripping down the steep hill. It was lucky that they didn't fall and tumble the whole way down. When they reached the waterfall, Lyzette remembered the first time Mikael had taken her here and how exciting it was.

He lay the blanket down on the ground and pushed her gently onto her back.

"This shirt is tight," he said, running his hands over her. He stopped to pay particular attention to her breasts. He made her suck in a ragged gasp. "You knew that bun would drive me crazy."

He pulled the shirt off, revealing a black lace bra with a front clasp. He stared at it.

"Honey, if I didn't know you better, I'd think you were hoping to get laid tonight," he said, with a wicked gleam in his eye.

"Maybe I was," she said, putting her hand on the bulge in his pants.

He undid the clasp of the bra and freed her breasts. Her bare nipples were stiff and throbbing.

His head dipped slowly to tease her. He licked all around until she groaned in frustration. Then and only then did he taste her, flicking her with his tongue and sucking until she felt mad with lust.

She undid his zipper, and he pulled his pants and underwear off, as well as his shirt, kneeling again beside her with his cock near her face. She wrapped her hand around its thick length, getting up to kneel before him. She licked up the underside and smiled to hear his harsh breathing. Then she took him into her mouth, moving up and down. She loved the taste of him, and it was driving her desire even higher. Mikael pushed her away.

"It's too much, Lyz, I'll come," he panted.

"Not before me," she said, straddling him. Slowly, she accepted him into her depths as she eased herself down onto his cock. When she was completely impaled, and they were hip to hip, she stayed there, resting her forehead against his.

They were both breathing in fits and starts. Lyzette finally began to move up and down on him. The angle was perfect, and she felt him hitting her G-spot over and over. She took it slow, wanting to savor it. Sometimes she came so fast she felt like she missed all the anticipation.

Mikael gazed into her eyes as she rose and fell before him.

"You are beautiful," he whispered. "I am lucky to have a sex goddess like you seducing me."

"I seduced you?" she panted. "You're the one dragging me into the bushes and making Jol wait."

She increased the pace, and he lifted her breasts to his mouth, bringing her closer to orgasm. Lyzette shifted her hips and felt her pelvis grinding on his, stimulating her clit with each thrust.

"Oh yeah, Lyzzie," he said, beginning to thrust up every time she slid down.

She didn't say anything as her climax slammed into her body. She flooded with ecstasy, and she wrapped her arms around Mik, holding on as the shuddering spasms shook her again and again.

He groaned and pounded into her frantically. He stiffened and filled her with his seed as she continued to shake violently with the powerful orgasm.

"Mik," she whispered in his ear, still breathing hard. "I love you."

"I love you, too, Lyzzie. You own me. I'm forever yours."

If you enjoyed this book, please review it on Amazon. Your review helps me succeed as an author.

To stay up-to-date on my latest releases, sign up for my newsletter at:

http://lisalace.com/newsletter/

# OTHER BOOKS BY LISA LACE

## WATER WORLD CONFIDENTIAL: A TERRAMATES NOVEL

He needed a wife. I wanted an alien lover.

The first time I saw Jori, I hated everything about him. He didn't care about anything except himself. On the other hand, his body was spectacular, and his muscles were firm. I couldn't stop thinking about him.

When TerraMates gave me the chance to marry Jori, I took it. I knew I needed the money. What I didn't know was that Jori's exterior was a facade, and he had kept secrets from everyone his entire life.

## ALIEN KISSES AND HOLIDAY WISHES

This captivating bundle includes six ALL-NEW stand-alone spicy hot holiday romances that celebrate the true meaning of the season - escaping with hot sexy aliens. Grab a cup of hot chocolate, sit back and relax with Amazon's bestselling sci-fi romance authors.

- Ashley West
- Pixie Moon
- Crystal Dawn
- Calista Skye
- Lucy Varna
- Lisa Lace

Preorder today to give yourself an early present for the holidays!

## CAPTURED BY THE ALIEN KING

When I saw my chance to get off Earth, I took it. I knew I needed to escape.

I didn't know I'd be claimed by an alien monarch in the middle of his mating season! Now we're on the run together, facing terrorists and natural disasters.

I'm still trying to figure out my feelings for this sexy guy. He is totally into me, but he has some unique ideas about alien romance...